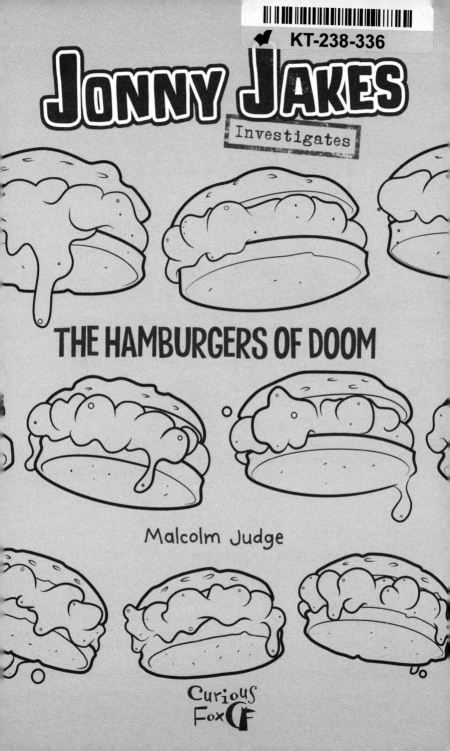

JONNY JAKES

Investigates

THE HAMBURGERS OF DOOM

Malcolm Judge

Curious Fox

To Kate, Mum, Gregory,
Elliot and Ollie

I'm Jonny Jakes.

That's not my real name.

When you're an undercover journalist you don't use your own name. If you're deep undercover you don't even use your own hair.

I have three spy cameras, fifteen disguises and more wigs than is normally considered healthy for a boy of my age.

I'm the reporter for
The Woodford Word.
Some people call it the
unofficial school
newspaper.

I call it ten pages of
truth and justice.

Mr Hardy, our head teacher, thinks *The Woodford Word* is 'scurrilous, misleading and unsuitable for young minds'.

That's the thanks you get for telling it like it is.

He's offering a reward of one hundred house points for any information that might lead to the unmasking of Jonny Jakes or the mysterious editor of the paper, Fiona Friend.

My other name is Fiona Friend.

If you want to read about how the school 'allows pupils' creativity to flourish in a supportive environment' then pick up the school's glossy prospectus. It's got a picture on the front of the Head Boy pretending to laugh at one of Mr Hardy's jokes.

If you want to know how the school really works then pick up a paper.

Mr Hardy would much rather you picked up a prospectus.

He doesn't like me.

I think some of my headlines might have offended him:

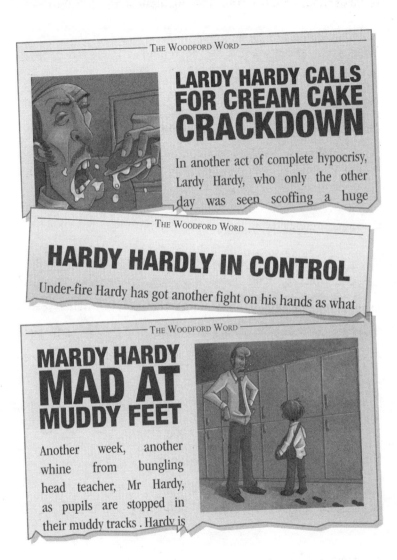

THE WOODFORD WORD

LARDY HARDY CALLS FOR CREAM CAKE CRACKDOWN

In another act of complete hypocrisy, Lardy Hardy, who only the other day was seen scoffing a huge

THE WOODFORD WORD

HARDY HARDLY IN CONTROL

Under-fire Hardy has got another fight on his hands as what

THE WOODFORD WORD

MARDY HARDY MAD AT MUDDY FEET

Another week, another whine from bungling head teacher, Mr Hardy, as pupils are stopped in their muddy tracks . Hardy is

To be honest, I can see why.

Not all of my headlines are about Mr Hardy. After all, *The Woodford Word* is there to provide the school population with balanced reporting about every aspect of school life.

It's just that Mr Hardy asks for it.

Take today. Up until last week Mr Hardy's bald patch was big enough to blind low-flying aircraft. This morning he walked in with shiny black hair.

So I'm going with:

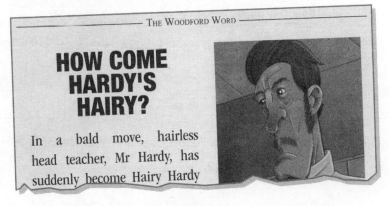

I mean, what am I supposed to do? Pretend it didn't happen? My readers need integrity. I'm a defender of truth and justice.

And I've got a paper to sell.

Hardy went ballistic.

He ordered bag searches across the whole school.
Normally I'm pretty careful but today I had some new
material for the paper badly hidden in my Geography
textbook.

I was in English when it happened, Mrs McKeane's
class. I'm good at English. I just try to make sure Mrs
McKeane never finds out.

I was sat next to Norris. Norris Morris. He's only
eleven and already he's the biggest boy in the school.
Which is a good job considering his name.

Mrs McKeane announced that she would be inspecting
our bags, row by row, and anyone found with anything
they shouldn't have would be sent straight to the Head.
She was very thorough. Books were shaken, bags were
turned upside down and every copy of *The Woodford
Word* was removed and thrown into a black bin bag.

I was trapped.

I stole a look beneath the table. My bag was open and there, sticking out of *The Planet We Live On*, was the picture I'd taken of Miss Frustup's rear bumper. Her car had mysteriously got a dent in it at exactly the same time as the *NO ENTRY* sign at the front of school got knocked over.

All the teachers were blaming it on 'local youths' but I knew different.

THE WOODFORD WORD

FRUSTUP'S BUSTUP

Felicity Frustup, Woodford's fussiest Maths teacher, seems to have got her own angles wrong this time

It was investigative journalism at its finest and it was about to get me chucked out of school.

Next to my bag, by a pair of huge feet, was Norris's bag. It was also open. I looked up. Mrs McKeane was getting closer. Trying not to think about the operation I would need if Norris's boots ever connected with my backside, I reached beneath the desk and slid my textbook and its deadly contents into Norris's bag.

Mrs McKeane reached our row of tables. She raked her bitter and twisted eyes over us. I tried to act normal but she was staring so hard everyone was starting to look like they'd done something wrong.

Everyone, that is, except Norris.

Norris smiled.

Norris always smiles. That's why everyone thinks he's thick.

Mrs McKeane thought Norris was thick, that's why he was on the back row with me. I could see what she was thinking. Why waste time searching the bags of intellectual pond life when none of us would be able to read *The Woodford Word*, let alone write it?

With a cluck of her tongue she made up her mind. She spun on her heel and headed back to her favourites at the front of the class and Act 3 Scene 5 of *Romeo and Juliet.*

I was free to write again another day.

I'd completely forgotten about Norris until a large hand tapped me on the shoulder at lunch break.

I turned around slowly. My eyes drew level with a large, white-shirted stomach. I looked up to see a bristly chin and the twin black holes of two giant nostrils. Although it was hard to tell from the angle I was looking from, I was pretty sure Norris was smiling.

I had no idea if that was a good sign or a bad sign.

Norris reached into his blazer pocket and began to pull out some rolled-up paper. It looked very familiar. I said goodbye to the world and shut my eyes.

When nothing happened I opened my eyes again. Norris's smile had grown even bigger than normal.

'"Frustup's Bustup". Nice one,' the giant boy said.
Then he winked a huge eyelid and strode off across the playground.

It's amazing I've got through the day without a change of underwear.

Wednesday 17th October
World Kindness Day
But apparently we still have to go to school.

Hardy's on his way out! He's had enough.

I haven't even been here a whole term.

I found out waiting for the nurse. I'm an expert at waiting for the nurse. No one bothers me. I put my head in my hands and make a sort of moaning sound. It's like you're invisible.

The great thing about waiting for the nurse is that you get to overhear everything Mrs Singh says. She's Mr Hardy's secretary in the next office along. She's so loud you could probably overhear her in the next postal district.

I get most of my stories waiting for the nurse and accidentally overhearing Mrs Singh.

As I held my stomach and made the occasional groan I could hear Mrs Singh on the phone. I'm still not convinced she actually needs one. Her door was closed and I could tell she was trying to keep her voice down but I still heard more than enough.

... take out an advert ... needs to include an interview date ... application forms available from...

And the clincher:

... salary of £80,000.

Only one job at Woodford School earns that sort of money.

It's time for a special issue.

I can't decide on a headline, there are so many to choose from:

> ## HARDY HITS THE HIGHWAY

or

> ## HAPPY END TO HARDY HORROR

or

> ## NO MORE HARDY, LET'S PARTY!

I could use the picture I took of the Year Nines waving goodbye from the back of the coach on their way to the Residential. It's perfect. They've got their faces squashed up against the window and they're waving with their thumbs in their ears.

I could have a Classic Quotes section from Mr Hardy's assemblies, including my all-time favourite:

'This school is a happy school, a caring school, and if I ever find out who stole our framed "Happy Child" Gold Star certificate from outside the canteen then I'll make them wish they'd never been born.'

But that's only two pages.

I need someone to help me
find some more material.
Someone who won't arouse
suspicion. Someone who won't
give me away. Someone who
won't mind using a silly name.

One particular someone springs
to mind.

Thursday 18th October

The good news is that the special edition notched up
record sales.

The bad news is if I wasn't Public Enemy Number One
before, I sure am now.

The teachers are mad I've found out about Hardy
leaving before them. Mr Hardy's mad because the
teachers are mad. And now the parents have gone mad.

They think *The Woodford Word* has become a menace. They think the school is out of control. They're demanding that Jonny Jakes and Fiona Friend be silenced immediately.

I don't want to be silenced.

Everyone's trying to catch me out. Teachers are patrolling everywhere, there are random bag checks all the time and the photocopier rooms are locked after every use.

I'm going to have to be careful.

Mrs McKeane keeps looking at me in a strange way. Maybe I got carried away with my essay on *Romeo and Juliet* and forgot to put in enough mistakes. Maybe she's wondering how *The Woodford Word* found out about her forgetting the silent 't' in Mr De Toillet's name last week.

Or maybe I've got GUILTY written all over my face.

Fortunately no one suspects Norris. No one ever suspects Norris. He just keeps smiling at everyone.

He must be the only pupil that hasn't had his bag
checked so he's keeping loads of photos for me. I might
not be getting a paper out anytime soon but when I
do I'm going to have plenty to say about this brutal
suppression of free speech.

I'm thinking:

TEACHERS CAN'T TAKE THE TRUTH

Or maybe even.

TRUTH TRAMPLED IN TERRIFYING
REIGN OF TEACHER TERROR

Although that's probably overdoing the Ts.

And then there's the damage to the business. The loyalty
of my customers. Too many bag searches and they'll
turn on me.

Or they would do if they knew who I was.

No paper equals no profit. No profit equals no more
disguises. No more disguises means no more wigs.

I must be strong.

Someone else wants to join *The Woodford Word*.

Norris found the Post-it note stuck under a teacher's desk in French. The undersides of the French teachers' desks are the communication network of the entire student population. I mean, when was the last time you saw a French teacher look closely at the bottom of their own desk?

Exactly.

> Dear Fiona Friend,
> Would like to help.
> Please leave instructions
> here tomorrow a.m.
>
> Justin Case

It could be a trap. Mr Hardy's always trying to catch me out. I'll set Justin Case a challenge. I'll ask him to wait for the nurse and see if he can find out the names of people applying for Hardy's job.

It's about time someone else was ill.

Just to be safe, I'll get Norris to put a reply under a different desk. If Justin Case is serious he'll find it, if he doesn't, he doesn't belong on *The Woodford Word*.

Turns out Justin Case *is* serious.

Norris left our note in period one and by break time he'd picked up a reply.

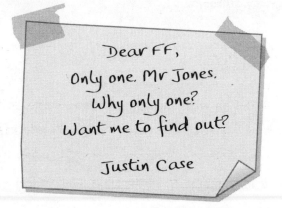

Dear FF,
Only one. Mr Jones.
Why only one?
Want me to find out?

Justin Case

Only one candidate for a job worth £80,000?

And Mr Jones? What sort of a name is that? That's the sort of name you use when you have to make up a false name.

I should know.

There's a story here, a big one. Too big to give to some idiot who calls themselves Justin Case.

Saturday 20th October
Falcon FX 3 released on Playstation.
Why am I so poor?

I'm in the bathroom.

We've got relatives.

I want to get on with the story but my Uncle Jack is determined to teach me how to play golf. He keeps making me swing an imaginary golf club round my head while he shouts at me to concentrate and keep my eye on

the imaginary ball. It's not going very well because all
I can think about is wrapping a non-imaginary golf club
around his non-imaginary stupid neck.

When I'm not being forced to play imaginary golf I'm
supposed to be playing with my two-year-old cousin.

He doesn't want to play with me.

He just wants to eat my ankles.

Sunday 21st October

See yesterday.

Monday 22nd October
Energy Saving Week
Dad won't have a problem with that.

As soon as I'd finished breakfast I went straight
round to Norris's house. We invented three people to

apply for Mr Hardy's job. I've got three accents.

There was Mr Knight from Scotland, Mr Roberts from Birmingham and Mr Parsons who was posh.

Norris made me practise. Mr Parsons sounded alright, Mr Roberts was a bit dodgy and Mr Knight kept going Indian. Luckily I didn't get to say much. All three conversations went exactly like this:

> Good morning, I'm Mr Knight/Roberts/ Parsons. I'd like an application form for the post of Head Teacher at Woodford School, please.

> I'm sorry sir, but the vacancy has already been filled. *Click.*

It was really weird for two reasons:

1 The advert in the paper had only just appeared and the final date for applications was two weeks away. Since when do you give someone the job and *then* advertise it?

2   (And this was the really weird one) Mrs Singh
    didn't want to chat.

Mrs Singh always wants to chat. She told me the entire
life story of her cat once.

I'd only asked her for a new planner.

So, not only is there just one person who has applied for
the job, it would seem the school only wants one person
for the job.

Who is this Mr Jones and what makes him so special?

Tuesday 23rd October
Take-A-Pet-To-Work day
Something else my parents refuse to get me.

Mr Jones is a hard man to track down.

I spent forty minutes with a funny pain in my elbow by
the main school office and didn't hear his name

mentioned once. Norris had a sprained nose for an hour and a half and he got nothing either.

More advanced research methods were needed.

Previous undercover investigations have revealed that, every day, at 2 p.m. precisely, Mrs Singh takes a big red bag of post across the playground to the post office opposite the school.

So, today at 1:59 and 55 seconds, a pupil who looked a bit like me, only with curly hair, three large spots and massive ears, threw a ball high into the air. As luck would have it, the ball happened to travel in the direction of the large double doors leading out from Reception to the playground.

Norris, a keen sportsman, was determined to take the catch and back pedalled quickly after the ball.

At 1:59 and 59 seconds Norris took a great catch.

At 2 p.m. precisely his backward momentum propelled him into a large-bosomed lady with a big red bag.

At 2 p.m. and 3 seconds I arrived on the scene to help.

I helped pick up letters to parents, I helped pick up payments for bills and I helped pick up order forms for stationery. I also picked up a small white envelope addressed to a Mr Jones, which I totally forgot to put back in the big red bag.

As everyone drifted back towards their form rooms at the end of break, Norris and I drifted towards the tin-roofed equipment store. Once we were safely out of sight I took off my disguise and got the white envelope out of my pocket.

I knew that you could use steam from kettles to open sealed envelopes without it looking too dodgy, but I didn't have a kettle so I tried breathing on it instead. I hadn't got very far when Norris snatched the envelope out of my hands and ripped it in half.

'Norris, what the...' I stammered, eyes out on stalks.

Then Norris stamped on the torn up envelope and smiled.

'What are you smiling at, you moron?' I shouted at him. In my panic I'd forgotten I was speaking to the biggest boy in the school.

Norris's smile widened and then he pretended to look innocent.

'Sorry, miss,' he said, putting on a goody-goody voice and perfect puppy-dog eyes. 'This must have fallen out of your bag. I think it must have got stuck on my boot.'

It took a moment or so to register but that's when I realized that Norris Morris, the stupid, smiling giant of Woodford School, was in fact a genius.

I joined the two halves of the letter, took a picture and then started to read.

Woodford School
West Woodford

Mr Jones
PO Box 4571
London

Dear Mr Jones,

Thank you for your gracious acceptance of the post of Head Teacher at Woodford School. I can't tell you how excited we all are. Everything is going smoothly. I look forward to meeting you in my office at 7:30 Thursday morning, as arranged, so we can make our final plans and I can answer any further questions you might have.

Yours sincerely,

Geoffrey Hardy

I was about to say something when a high-pitched voice behind me beat me to it.

'Give!'

We turned round. Michelle Bell, the hardest girl in school, held out her hand. There was a big gold ring on every finger. They weren't for decoration.

In our hurry we hadn't checked to make sure that we were alone. It was an unforgivable schoolboy error.

Even for schoolboys.

Michelle Bell wasn't alone. She never was. Trevor Neave fancied her, so he was sharing his chips.

'Oi! Hand it over. Or...' Trevor Neave paused for thought. He could barely speak in sentences, let alone write them. 'Else!' he managed eventually.

I had no problem handing over the letter. There wasn't exactly much to remember so why not let someone else run the risk of getting caught with it? Norris, however, had other ideas. I'd never seen him without a smile before now.

'Or else what?' he said in a steely voice.

Trevor Neave unwrapped his hairy arms from the tiny waist of Michelle Bell and squared up to Norris. He may have been stupid but he recognised a challenge to his position as school hard case when he saw it.

At any other time I would have happily stepped back and watched Norris pound Trevor Neave into a pulp, but we had bigger fish to fry. Besides, Jonny Jakes works better in the shadows and he was in serious danger of stepping into the limelight.

Trevor Neave was winding himself up for another attempt at intelligent speech but I saved him the effort.

'Have it,' I said, holding the letter towards him. 'Be my guest. We'll leave you to it.'

I pulled at Norris's sleeve but he was failing to grasp the idea of not drawing attention to ourselves. He was failing to grasp it in a spectacular way.

'He's not having it,' Norris said, snatching the letter out of my hand again. He was red in the face. 'We need this, it's too important. We need it for the paper...'

To be fair, as soon as he'd said it, he realized what he'd done. Unfortunately he was one word too late.

Michelle Bell placed her bright-red fingernails on Trevor Neave's shoulder and gently pulled him out of the way. She had a vicious-looking smile on her face.

'The paper?' she trilled, annoyingly. 'So, you squirts work for *The Woodford Word*? How interesting.'

I thought about trying to deny it but Norris's face was a complete giveaway. I did the next best thing, I kept quiet. Better her thinking we were a tiny cog in the machine rather than her knowing that we *were The Woodford Word*.

'Cat caught your tongue?' she continued, spinning a blob of bubble gum around her mouth. 'Well that's okay, squirts, I'll do the talking for you. You tell Fiona Friend that I want my own fashion page. It's about time that paper had something decent in it. Tell her I want a double page with glossy pictures and fashion advice. And tell her I want to be called ... Chella. Do you think you can remember all that, squirts?'

I nodded.

I tried to bite my tongue.

It didn't work.

'And what if Fiona Friend tells you to go and stick your head down a toilet?'

Michelle Bell leaned in close. I could barely breathe for perfume.

'Then tell her,' she whispered, 'that if I don't see myself in print by the end of this week, two of her reporters will be expelled.'

And with those kind words she left, pulling her boyfriend along by his tie.

Norris stared at the muddy paper in his hands. He looked like he'd never smile again.

Wednesday 24th October
Switzerland becomes independent 1648
I've still got to wait another seven years.

I need to get *The Woodford Word* out by Friday or I'm history.

The problem is the teachers are absolutely everywhere, marching up and down the corridors, invading the playground and generally lurking around every corner. My bag gets searched about five times a day and if Mrs McKeane stares at me any harder she's going to go cross-eyed.

Norris hasn't been much help. I can't get a word out of him. I've tried encouragement and I've tried shouting at him. As a last resort I tried hitting him but I don't think he even noticed. He's like a zombie. If he doesn't start smiling soon he's going to get his bag inspected along with the rest of us.

Then, even if I do get the paper out, it's got to have a double-page fashion feature put together by someone who wouldn't know fashion if it jumped out and catwalked across her face.

The one consolation is the Mr Jones letter.

It's quite a big consolation. Intrigue, conspiracy and double dealing, it doesn't get much better than that. And guess where I'm going to be 7:30 tomorrow morning?

 Thursday 25th November

At last. The story that will make me a legend.

This time I'm not just going to make the headlines. I'm going to *be* the headlines.

World domination of the media ☑

I left early. Mum wasn't even awake. I put a note under her door telling her I'd probably be late back because I had loads of homework I needed to finish at school. She falls for it every time.

Me and Norris had to find a good hiding place before
the meeting. For a whole half term I'd been skulking
around the corridor outside Hardy's office. Today I was
going in.

Our disguises were simple but effective: boiler suits and
baseball hats. We could have been loading up the drinks
machine, moving some furniture or cleaning the drains.
No one would give us a second look and the peaks on our
caps meant our faces wouldn't be seen by the CCTV
cameras trained on the school entrance.

As luck would have it, Hardy's door was unlocked. It
was a big wooden door and creaked dramatically as we
pushed it open. I reckon he deliberately doesn't oil the
hinges.

I put my finger on my lips and we went in.

Our luck stopped as soon as it started. Mr Hardy's office is the most boring office in the world. Apart from the hideous wallpaper there's just a big desk, three chairs and a steel cupboard.

The steel cupboard might have worked but it was locked and we couldn't find the key. We tried hiding under the desk but Norris kept lifting it up with his massive butt.

As Norris crawled back out from under the desk he pointed to his watch to show me that we were running out of time.

I pointed to his huge backside to explain why our plan was experiencing a little difficulty.

He did a little mime to suggest that we got up on the roof so that he could lower me down to see through the top of Mr Hardy's window.

I did a little mime to show him that I'd completely forgotten to bring my climbing rope with me.

Norris did a mime back that suggested I was a big girly chicken and that if I didn't get up the drainpipe right now he was going to tell everyone.

I started to do a mime back but Norris didn't like it and made me stop.

We legged it back outside and scrambled up the drainpipe Matthew Robinson uses when the bigger boys make him get their footballs off the roof. No sooner were we up on the tiles when we heard a car rumble up the drive.

It was Hardy. He got out directly below us. He was making a real effort for his mysterious visitor. The wig was freshly washed and as we peeked a little further over the edge of the roof we could almost see our reflection in his highly polished shoes.

Minutes later another car arrived. Something was odd about it.

I tried to work out what was so weird. Was it too black? Was it too quiet? Or was it because it didn't seem to completely make contact with the road?

I looked at Norris. He was as puzzled as me.

The car silently pulled to a halt next to Hardy's. I still didn't recognise the make. There was no badge or name on it. And there were no lines on it either, nothing to help you tell the difference between the doors or the bonnet or the windscreen. It looked like it was made from a solid piece of pure black.

A door opened. Norris and I held our breaths. At last we were going to see our mysterious new head teacher. A brown shoe stepped out on the tarmac, then another.

Then another.

But, before we could see any more, Mr Hardy blocked our view by putting an umbrella over his guest and whisking him inside. I'd been too stunned to take a photograph until it was too late. All I got was the top of the umbrella.

My heart was racing. I held up three fingers to Norris, just to check my brain hadn't made it up. He held up three fingers back and nodded.

Once we'd given them a little time to get settled, Norris grabbed my ankles and carefully lowered me head-first over the edge of the roof. The blood rushed to my head and I could feel Norris trembling with the effort of holding me. I should have been scared but the smell of a big story has a way of keeping me focused.

Inch by inch, my eyes drew level with the top edge of Mr Hardy's window. My eyes widened. If I hadn't been held upside down by the biggest boy in the school I'd have fainted with the shock.

I'm not quite sure how to say this so I'm just going to come straight out with it.

... It's probably best to sit down.

Mr Jones is an alien.

I know. It still sounds weird to me and I saw it. I've been practising saying it in my head all day.

Mr Jones is an alien.

Still weird.

But he is. Either that or the human race has just evolved into three-legged, purple-headed, five-eyed beings and I just didn't notice.

And this time I did get the picture.

I think it's safe to say we've got a front page.

I made sure Norris put me down safely before I told him what I'd seen. I had to tell him quite a few times.

He wanted to have a look for himself but I wasn't about to try and dangle him off the edge of a building, so he had to make do with the photograph I'd taken. Eventually it seemed to sink in.

Mr Jones's exit was as quick as his arrival. Mr Hardy held the umbrella over his head again, despite the bright sunshine. As far as the pair of them were concerned they'd had a secret meeting.

They'll soon find out they hadn't.

We spent the rest of the morning in a daze. I think I might even have smiled at Michelle Bell as she handed over *The Woodford Word*'s new fashion feature. It had lots of pictures of her friends trying on dresses with too many straps.

By lunchtime I'd managed to clear my head a little so I turned my attention to how we were actually going to get the paper out. Online has never been an option. I never know when I'm going to get banned. Besides, the internet speed at school makes the average snail look like a Formula One racing car.

Trying to get to a photocopying room would be impossible, they were much too heavily guarded. We needed to get hold of lots of printer ink and paper and then find a nice, quiet room with a computer, a scanner and a printer. It had to be somewhere nobody ever goes and we'd have to stay in the room for a very long time.

Which is why we're still in the PC study room.

Friday 26th October

By the end of today I should have been rich and famous beyond my wildest dreams - and I've got some pretty wild dreams.

Norris and I had everything ready. We had worked through the night, and by the time we heard the Site Manager doing his early morning rounds there were five hundred copies of *The Woodford Word* ready to gobsmack the world.

We'd kept the headline simple but we'd put it twice:

THE WOODFORD WORD

NEW HEAD OF WOODFORD SCHOOL IS AN ALIEN
NEW HEAD OF WOODFORD SCHOOL IS AN ALIEN

After all, with a story like that and a picture to back it up, what else did we need?

We sneaked out of the PE study room with our bundles of papers. Yesterday Norris had put a note under Madame Angerie's desk to let everyone know that, despite the ongoing danger of our secret identities being revealed, we had a story that just had to be told. It informed pupils that copies of *The Woodford Word* would be available first thing Friday morning from lockers 501 and 502, and this time we didn't even want paying.

We didn't notice anything at first. But when we saw our first clock I realized something was up. It was 8:35 and it was quiet.

Too quiet.

We listened carefully for signs of life. There was a
faint hum coming from the direction of the main hall.
Every now and then it would rise up before bubbling
under again.

Norris and I started to walk towards it.

As we got closer the sound changed. It was more broken
up and getting louder. It was the sound of voices,
hundreds of voices, all chattering at the same time.
Sometimes the voices would gather into a wave of noise,
and when it did, we could make out cheers and clapping.

Something big was going on. I got a funny feeling in
the pit of my stomach and it had nothing to do with
missing breakfast.

I happened to look out of one of the corridor windows
and saw a row of white vans parked along the school
drive. They had aerials and satellite dishes sticking out
the top of them.

That wasn't usual.

I looked closer and saw cameras and lots of people with headphones talking to lots of other people with headphones. There were even a couple of helicopters circling above.

By the time we got to the main hall the sound had reached fever pitch. Norris managed to push open the double doors just wide enough for us to slip in amongst the excited crowd.

Everyone was trying to get a view of the stage. I could see some of the pupils in my year sitting on top of their dads' shoulders and every window ledge and every chair was being stood on. I could hardly see a thing. One of Norris's more useful skills as an undercover reporter is that he's strong enough to let you stand on his shoulders while he grabs your legs.

On the stage was a single microphone lit by a single spotlight. Just when it seemed the noise couldn't get any louder, there was a violent shushing sound as everyone put their fingers to their lips. Mr Hardy came on the stage. He tried his best to look serious but you could tell he was loving all the attention.

He waited until every last whisper had died away before he began to speak.

'Ladies and gentlemen, welcome to Woodford School. As you know, the school has always been at the cutting edge of education and today is no different.

'Today, we break more boundaries and tread new ground. Children, parents, ladies and gentlemen of the press, I'm afraid we have been keeping a little secret from you. Indeed, we've been keeping it from the rest of the world. A secret that even *The Woodford Word* hasn't managed to uncover.'

He left a pause for dramatic effect. I wanted to shout something out but my throat was completely dry. This wasn't supposed to happen.

'Today, Woodford School begins a project that will pave the way for the teaching of tomorrow.'

Mr Hardy paused again. He'd spent a lot of time coming up with that.

'We've been doing our own homework and through our extensive search for a new head teacher we've discovered that, in order to provide our children with a world-class education, we needed something that's, well, a little out of this world.'

The funny feeling at the pit of my stomach was feeling less funny all the time and my brain had turned into syrup. My world exclusive was about to slip through my fingers, and all I could do was stand there and take it.

Mr Hardy was working up to his finale.

'Ladies and gentlemen, I never thought I'd be the one to tell you, indeed to tell the world, that we are not alone in the universe, but it is my great honour

to introduce you to a teacher who has come a very long way indeed to be with us today. A teacher whose skills have been honed in classrooms not just across the country but across the cosmos. A teacher who not only knows the square root of pi but uses it to steer his spacecraft. Ladies and gentlemen, from the *universally* respected Edu K8 Foundation on planet Huurl please welcome ... Mr Jones.'

And there he was.

All three legs, five eyes and purple head of him.

And in lockers 501 and 502, five hundred newspapers became yesterday's news.

Saturday 26th October
Where's the end of the world when you need it?

Yesterday I had the chance to break the biggest news story since dinosaurs were wiped off the face of the Earth.

I blew it.

Mr Jones's face is everywhere. You can't move for hearing his name. You know when something really important has happened when everyone forgets to talk about the weather.

He's all over the TV, all over the radio, and the internet is in serious risk of meltdown. What makes it worse is that most of the time Hardy's there too. Last week he was on the front of *The Woodford Word* stuffing his face with a doughnut, now he's on the cover of the *New York Times* with his arm round Mr Jones, smiling like he's just won a year's supply of HobNobs.

I think I'm going to have to spend the rest of my life under a rock.

Sunday 27th October

I haven't left my bedroom all weekend.

Mum's been trying to tempt me out with cake. She says

I'll feel better for a bit of fresh air and the chance for a chat.

Dad keeps knocking on the door and asking me to turn the awful music down. I can't believe I'm related to someone who doesn't appreciate the musical genius of The Pain Cradle.

Norris called round to say I should be pleased with how close we got to the story of a lifetime. He said I've got a great future ahead of me and I should stop sulking and pull myself together.

I told him to go away and stop talking like my parents.

Monday 28th October

First, you find out your new head teacher is an alien.

Then, your old head teacher tells the world about it just before you do and ruins the rest of your life. Then, as if things weren't bad enough, the new head teacher calls a 'Special Assembly' in the gym which means you have to sit on a cold wooden floor and get talked at. For an hour.

Mr Jones came in to the hall accompanied by a barrage of flash photography from the world's press who haven't found anything better to do with themselves yet. He was wearing the same stuff as before: brown suit, brown and white striped tie, white shirt, brown trousers and brown shoes. I don't know if he thinks that's what an Earth teacher should wear or whether the rest of the universe just has no style.

Up close, you could see that his five eyes were able to look in five different directions at once and that he smelt slightly of dishwater. He fitted right in with the Chemistry Department.

But the worst thing about it wasn't the press, or his smell, or my numb bum on the cold floor. It wasn't even his appalling fashion sense.

The worse thing about it was that he was so nice.

He started with a little bit of 'firm but fair' and 'running a tight ship' but then he started apologizing that we hadn't been told about him before. He said that he'd asked Mr Hardy if he could let the pupils know as soon as the school had first contacted him but he'd been persuaded not to. He hoped he could 'earn our trust' in the weeks to follow. He showed us where his home planet was and some pictures of other schools in other galaxies that he'd worked in. He showed us a picture of his personal spaceship and some pictures of his children.

He's got seventy-three.

He kept saying 'what a privilege' it was to be here and how much he was looking forward to 'our learning together'. At the end he even offered everyone some sweets.

It was so bad I almost wished Mr Hardy was back.

When it was all over I tried standing up but my brain had forgotten what my legs did, so I just stayed where I was. Everyone else looked pretty dazed too as they wandered out to morning break. Some kids even waited around to ask him questions.

Mr Jones smiled patiently and answered them all, one by one.

I hate him.

I don't know how long I was like that, just sitting and staring and wishing I could wipe the stupid triangular smile off his stupid purple face. If Norris hadn't poked me in the ribs I'd probably still be there now.

I'm depressed.

I'm spending so much time in my bedroom I've started naming the furniture.

Tuesday 29th October
The anniversary of the start of the Great Depression
I know how they felt.

Justin Case is at it again.

Norris brought me a note at lunchtime.

Dear FF,
Why didn't you get back to me?
I found his name out in the first place
didn't I? We could have got this story
first. We'd have been famous!
Thanks for nothing!

JC

It was good to know someone else was in a bad mood
but it didn't help cheer me up.

Wednesday 30th October

I must be bad. I heard Mum ask if Dad could have a
father-and-son talk with me about how my body was
changing and how to control my emotions.

I hope he keeps it short.

Norris brought me three more notes from Justin Case
today; they kind of have a theme.

Dear FF,

I didn't mean to get angry, it's just I'm sure we could make a good team, that's all. Look, I've found out something else that you'll find interesting. Get back to me by lunchtime and I might just let you in on a little secret!

JC

FF,

So you're just going to ignore me now are you? Well don't think I'm going anywhere. If you won't keep up with the news then I will. If I don't get a note by the end of the day then *The Woodford Word* is history – I'll bring out my own paper.

JC

> Oi FF,
> or whatever your stupid name is.
> I mean it! You're either with me or
> against me!! I'm not bluffing!!!
>
> JC

He's bluffing.

If you're serious you don't need to use three
exclamation marks.

Thursday 31st October
Halloween
Definitely the last year my Dracula
costume's going to fit me.

The reporters are starting to drift off. It's all
very well reporting on the arrival of the first extra-
terrestrial life form but it's difficult to keep writing
articles about how nice he is. Mr Jones has been giving
them regular briefings. I've been to a few in disguise.

Someone made the mistake of asking him what it was like to teach human pupils. He went on about the joys of teaching ultra long division to the Year Eights, how the Year Tens were fascinated about learning the fundamentals of Huurlian grammar and what a thoroughly interesting game cricket is.

It's got to the stage where all they can be bothered to ask him is whether they can have any more of his sweets.

Friday 1st November

Everyone still loves Mr Jones. It's driving me mad. Okay, so he's got a brain the size of a planet and he's taught us more in a week than we've learnt in the whole of the rest of our education.

But that's not the point.

He's everywhere. You can't get away from him. He glides along the corridors and he's so quick and quiet it's unnerving.

I had my head in my locker today, getting my books out, and when I turned round he was there, right in front of me. Smiling.

He's worse than Norris for smiling.

He offered me one of his sweets and asked me if I was okay. I said I was fine, but I just had a funny tummy. His eyes were all full of understanding, or at least the three that I could see were. I thought for a second that he might have worked out who I was but he seemed genuinely upset that I didn't seem to be happy. I couldn't tell him my problem was staring me in the face.

I can't have teachers feeling sorry for me.

The Woodford Word must rise again.

Saturday 2nd November

I'm trying to do the paper. There's just one problem.

No news.

This week everything's been perfect. Everything's running on time. The school looks cleaner than it's ever looked. All the teachers are being nice and all the pupils are really happy.

Well, nearly all.

Why is everyone being so nice? Even Trevor Neave's managed to stop hitting people.

Other than having an alien for a head teacher, the only story is there is no story.

Sunday 3rd November

Mr Jones did one of those interviews-on-a-sofa type programmes on TV this morning. He was asked what he was enjoying most about life on Earth. He said he didn't think much of the weather but he couldn't believe how he'd managed to survive so long without a good cup of tea. The interviewer laughed his head off.

I nearly cried.

I'm starting a Mr Jones fact file. I might have to publish it if I can't find anything to put in the paper.

I'm brainstorming possible titles. The two I like at the moment are:

> # MR JONES
> ## The Truth About The Thing
> ## That Ruined My Life

or

> # EXTRATERRESTRIAL LIFE
> ## More Boring Than You
> ## Would Have Thought Possible

Monday 4th November

I knew Justin Case was bluffing.

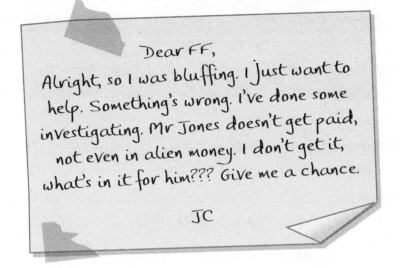

Dear FF,

Alright, so I was bluffing. I just want to help. Something's wrong. I've done some investigating. Mr Jones doesn't get paid, not even in alien money. I don't get it, what's in it for him??? Give me a chance.

JC

I don't like his name and I certainly don't like his excessive use of punctuation, but Justin Case is making a habit of coming up with the good stuff.

I don't get it either. Who travels halfway across the universe out of the goodness of his heart, especially when he's got seventy-three mouths to feed?

Maybe I should give Justin Case a chance. I can't afford not to have the sort of information he keeps coming up with.

It's a good job I've finally got some sort of story. Michelle Bell cornered me outside my locker at break.

She was a bit calmer than usual but still wanted to know what had happened to her fashion feature.

I tried to explain that Fiona Friend *had* put her fashion feature in the last edition of *The Woodford Word*, but when Mr Jones came along no one had wanted to buy it. That only started to wind her up again. So then I tried to point out that it was really hard to get a paper out at the moment because everyone was being so nice to each other.

I've got three days to sort it out or something horrible is going to happen to my leg.

Tuesday 5th November
Bonfire Night
Nothing to live for now until Christmas.

I left a note for Justin Case explaining how our business relationship would work.

JC,

If you want to help *The Woodford Word*,
stop using too much punctuation or I'll make
it my mission in life to reveal your true
identity and take you down.

FF

P.S. Dig deeper.

Then Norris and I went alien-tracking.

We watched Mr Jones's every move.

We stalked him down the corridors and saw him ask
some Year Tens to tuck in their shirts. We spied on
him in the staffroom with a camera we'd hidden behind
the teachers' pigeonholes and heard him ask Mrs Flynn
how her mother was. We watched through the window
in the Music corridor as he patrolled the playground and
kicked a football back to Simon Huck after he'd missed
a penalty.

We saw him do nothing suspicious whatsoever.

By the end of the day I was exhausted and beginning to think I should forget the whole thing. Maybe I'd got it all wrong. Maybe it's just humans who don't do anything without expecting something in return.

I was following Mr Jones down the millionth corridor of the day and wasn't concentrating. I'd got much too close. Suddenly he turned round unexpectedly and I nearly walked straight into him.

'Sorry, sir, I wasn't looking where I was going,' I spluttered. My heart was pounding, I was sure he must have worked out he was being followed. He had enough eyes. But Mr Jones hardly seemed to notice I was there. He was sucking hard on something in his mouth.

'Don't worry, dear boy, don't worry,' he murmured in a distracted sort of way. 'Here, have a sweet,' he said cheerfully and offered me his bag of sweets.

That's when it hit me. We'd followed him all day and he'd given a sweet to everyone he'd met.

Most head teachers don't do that sort of thing.

Slowly, I joined my thoughts up:

1   Mr Jones has been giving out sweets from the moment he arrived.

2   Ever since he arrived, everyone's been acting weirdly nice.

3   Something in the sweets is making everyone act weirdly nice.

4   Eating Mr Jones's sweets would be a really bad idea for an undercover reporter who needs to stay focused on being a defender of truth and justice.

Luckily I hadn't had any yet. I don't take sweets from strangers, and I certainly don't take them from aliens who've helped destroy my chances of becoming rich and famous beyond my wildest dreams. I'd banned Norris from having any too on principle. It hadn't gone down well but he'd thank me now.

The bag of sweets came closer. They had a powerful, honey-like smell that made your head spin. I got the strangest desire to jump inside the bag and swim around in their sugar-coated loveliness.

'No, thank you,' I said as politely as I could manage.

Mr Jones was alert in an instant. Most of his eyes stopped whatever it was they were doing and turned to look at me. I felt like an amoeba under a microscope.

'Everyone else likes them,' he said, pulling at his lower lip thoughtfully. It wasn't pleasant.

I needed an excuse. I'm good at excuses. I've normally got hundreds of them. But at that moment they all vanished from my mind. Mr Jones continued to examine me.

Finally an excuse came along. It wasn't good but it would have to do. Mr Jones's stare was about to crumble me into a pile of dust.

'I've got to go, sir, it's er ... my cat's birthday.'

And with that masterpiece I turned and forced myself to walk calmly to the end of the corridor. I could feel Mr Jones's stare, like five red-hot pinpricks, burning into my back the whole time.

As soon as I got round the corner and out of sight I legged it all the way home.

I told my parents about Mr Jones and the sweets.

They said I had an overactive imagination. They said I should give him a chance and that I just needed a little time to adjust to his methods.

I said what was the point telling them about my problems when they wouldn't take me seriously.

They said I was jumping to conclusions.

I said they should go and jump in a lake.

That's when they sent me to my room.

They came up later for
a 'chat'. Dad sat on my
bed and talked in that
stupid way he does when
he thinks he's treating
me like an adult. Mum
sat next to him and
nodded but I know she
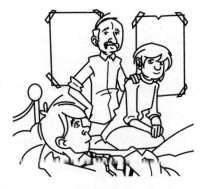
hates the voice too. I can tell by the way she grinds her
teeth.

She took over and said they were glad I'd come to them
with my concerns and, if it made me feel better, they
would promise not to eat any of Mr Jones's sweets.

I thanked her for her concern, but as she left I caught
her giving Dad one of her winks.

I'd take the voice over the wink any day.

We're in big trouble. The sweets are making everyone in school go round with a big smile on their face.

Even the teachers.

It's a really weird smile. It looks like it's been painted on by a four-year-old. Everyone's mouth is full of teeth. Their eyes are shiny but sort of glazed-over at the same time, like they're all trying too hard to look cheerful in a photograph.

I warned Justin Case about the sweets. He said he hasn't had any either as he's a diabetic. He hasn't got anything new on Mr Jones but he's as freaked out as I am about how everyone's behaving.

The Woodford Word has got to bring the school back to its senses. It's time to fire up the photocopier and go for some shock tactics. The headline's going to be:

WHAT ARE YOU LAUGHING AT?

I'm using an old picture of pupils in the playground:

It's good to know Art lessons haven't been a complete waste of time.

Thursday 7th November

Yesterday I thought we were in trouble.

Today made yesterday look like a walk in the park.

We didn't sell a single copy of *The Woodford Word*. We didn't even manage to give one away.

In the end we resorted to slipping copies into peoples' bags when they weren't looking but when they found them, they just picked them up, stared at them blankly and threw them in the bin. No one was interested.

Apart from Mr Jones.

He called an assembly for the whole school.

'Good morning, children,' he began. It didn't sound like he meant it.

'Good morning,' the grinning zombies chanted back.

'It has come to my attention that some of us are unhappy,' he continued, 'and if you're unhappy it makes me unhappy.' Mr Jones sighed for effect. For some reason everyone else did the same. Mr Jones held up *The Woodford Word* between what we would have called a thumb and a forefinger but which looked more like a stapler and a butter dish.

'I had been told about this paper before I arrived. As I'm sure you are aware, my predecessor, Mr Hardy, was not a fan of this newspaper and warned me to be on the lookout for the pupils responsible. Well, children, today I am on the lookout for those responsible. Not because I want to punish them, of course, but because I would like to talk with them, to listen to their concerns and to put their minds at ease.'

Something dark swam across the back of Mr Jones's eyes. He smiled harder.

'As you know, I like to recognise the achievements of everybody in the school and, if there are some of us who have a talent for...' he paused to make sure he chose the right words and I could tell he was trying to control his temper, '... for creative writing, then I would like to discuss how we can work together to develop that talent further.

'So, if Miss Friend or Mr Jakes - or indeed anyone else with a delightfully funny name - would like to come and visit me in my office, I'm sure we could sort out any problems. In the meantime I suggest we recycle Miss Friend's contribution in the paper recycling boxes I have just ordered for each classroom.'

All three corners of Mr Jones's mouth were quivering.

He was fighting his temper but his temper was winning.

He was starting to shout as he paced restlessly up and down the stage.

'Of course, if Mr Jakes or Miss Friend doesn't want to come forward then one of their friends might need to persuade them! Perhaps there is someone here now who would like to tell us who they really are! Come along, we haven't got all day!'

Mr Jones's normal, smooth movements had become jerky, and his whole barrel chest began heaving violently up and down. When he spoke again the words struggled to get out.

'The person who tells me ... gets ... a ... bag ... of SWWWEEEEEETS!'

Mr Jones was now completely out of control. His head was swelling, and as his pacing got faster and faster his breathing became louder and louder. It was deep and unpleasant and rattly, like someone brushing gravel down a drain.

Then another noise began to fill the hall, a loud, liquidy, pumping sound. The sound of Mr Jones's heartbeat.

Well, five heartbeats.

I never want to hear anything like it again.

Finally, just in case things weren't totally freaky enough, Mr Jones's eyes started to dart about.

Literally.

The smallest one moved first. The skin around it just seemed to swim out of the way as it went from his forehead to his chin. In a few moments all the eyes were whirling about, pulsating in time with the heartbeats and changing colour as they went.

The whole thing was having an effect on the students.

They started to sway on their feet, and their shoulders whipped backwards and forwards. I was so shocked I almost forgot to copy them.

Mr Jones stepped down from the stage. He started to inspect the rows of horribly shaking bodies.

When he got to Barry Devine, Mr Jones stopped. Something about him had caught his attention. He circled around him slowly, bent over him and ran his bulging nose up and down his arm. Barry's eyes stared straight ahead, unaware that he now had alien snot dripping off his sleeve.

I tried very hard not to puke.

Just when I felt like there was no holding it back, the doors at the side of the hall clattered open. Miss Briars, the drama teacher, backed in to the hall dragging a large table noisily behind her. Mr Jones's spell was instantly broken and one thousand two hundred and fifty-four pupils came back to their senses.

One of them discovered a disgusting new stain on his jumper.

Miss Briars had no idea what she had just walked into. She was halfway across the hall before she realized she wasn't alone. When she did, she fumbled for her glasses which were on a long piece of gold cord around her neck.

'Ah, sorry, er ... Headmaster. Ah ... pupils! School play auditions!' she said, pointing proudly at the table. Mr Jones didn't say anything. He was doing his best to start breathing properly again but his face was like a thunderstorm.

After a long, uncomfortable silence, Miss Briars eventually got the hint that perhaps now was not the time. 'Well, I'll, hum ... go back downstairs then. Everyone's welcome of course, spot of ... you know ... tread the boards, *et cetera*. Hmm ... ah ... right. Toodle-oo!'

Everyone turned to watch her go, which she did after colliding with a large bin.

When she had left, the whole school turned back to Mr Jones. A sea of vacant smiles waited for him to say something. They were disappointed.

I'm rethinking the fact-file idea. I'm thinking more like a survival guide. Something like:

A SURVIVAL GUIDE TO ALIENS AND HOW TO ESCAPE THEIR EVIL FIVE-EYED CLUTCHES

I gave my parents a second chance and told them about the assembly.

It was either that or phone the police, and I reckoned my parents were less likely to put me in a straitjacket and cart me off to a padded room.

This time they listened. They took me seriously. They said they'd take it up with the school first thing in the morning. Dad said I did the right thing in coming to them. Mum asked me if I was okay and if there was anything I wanted.

I was just beginning to think that they might actually be of some use for a change when they smiled. A shiver ran down my spine.

It was one of *those* smiles.

I asked them if they'd had any sweets. They said they hadn't, although Mr Jones had mentioned them in the meeting last night.

I said what meeting.

They said the 'Meet the Head' meeting all the mums and dads went to.

Goose pimples sprang up on my arm.

They said it was very interesting. They said several parents had asked about the sweets and Mr Jones had admitted he used them to help achieve a 'positive learning environment'. He also admitted that they had a slightly hypnotic quality.

He showed them pictures of how the sweets had helped control behaviour in other schools he'd taught at. They said he'd even admitted giving a few to the press as he'd been told they might make a nuisance of themselves and that it would help keep them in order.

They said that Mr Jones had made it very clear that the sweets would be phased out shortly once 'positive learning patterns have been thoroughly embedded.' The more they talked about him the bigger their smiles got.

I asked them again if they were sure they hadn't had any sweets.

They said no.

But the biscuits were lovely.

Friday 8th November

Norris's parents are the same.

He said that when he'd told them about the assembly they'd listened carefully, just like mine. He said they'd had a weird smile on their faces, just like mine. Then he said they'd given him a massive cuddle.

I'd been lucky.

I told Norris we had to send a note to Justin Case to see if he was still okay. I hadn't noticed anyone else who wasn't in a trance in the assembly. Hopefully that was because I'd been too busy acting like my brains had been sucked out.

Justin Case sent a note back saying he was okay but *he* thought *I'd* been got.

I sent a note telling him we were fine but our parents had been got.

He sent a note back saying his were the same and shouldn't we be contacting the authorities.

I sent a note back asking him if he knew the 'my head teacher is a mind-controlling alien' emergency contact number.

He sent a note back saying there's no need to be sarcastic.

Then Norris said he was sick of carrying notes about.

'You need to meet him,' he added.

'Why?'

'Well, what have we got to lose?' he asked, gulping down the can of Irn-Bru he'd got from the supermarket. 'At the moment it's three of us against all of them and we're spending our time swapping notes instead of actually doing something.'

He had a point. To celebrate he broke the seal on an extra large jar of crunchy peanut butter and dipped his finger in. We can only eat food we've got ourselves now.

I'm not confident Norris is going to have a balanced diet.

'But you need to hide your identities,' he said, spraying me with globules of brown paste.

'I thought you said we needed to meet each other?' I said.

'Yeah, but you don't want to see each other, do you?'

'What do you mean?'

'You don't want to actually see each other because, if you do and then one of you gets caught, you'll be made to grass the other one up. If you don't know who the other person is, you can't grass each other up.'

Norris had a point. That made two. He was on fire.

'And you'll have to meet in the girls' toilets,' he added.

He was an idiot.

'What do you mean "the girls' toilets"?' I demanded. 'Why would I want to meet Justin Case in the girls' toilets?'

'Because, you're supposed to be Fiona Friend,' he explained slowly, 'and that's a *girl's name*, isn't it?'

Norris grinned. He was right again and he was loving it.

That's why I stole his peanut butter.

Cooking sucks.

I told Mum I was doing a special survival project and had to look after myself all weekend.

I'm not sure I'm going to make it.

My spaghetti bolognese looked like I'd dropped one of my wigs in a cowpat and trodden on it. It didn't taste much better.

Mum keeps offering me biscuits. Mr Jones gave everyone a box of them at the parents' meeting. The smell's driving me crazy but if I eat one of them, I become one of *them*. It's like having a whole field of bubble wrap in front of you and being told you can't walk on it.

I've been trying to take my mind off the biscuits and the fact that I've got to go into the girls' toilets on Monday by doing some research on the internet. I need some help with the survival guide.

There were millions of pictures of 'aliens' but none of them wore brown suits. I put in 'evil alien teacher', but that just brought up loads of stuff about teachers setting too much homework. Then I put in 'Can anyone help me defeat an alien head teacher who is hypnotizing everyone with sweets and biscuits?'

There's some very strange people out there.

I've made an important editorial decision about the guide though. I need a new pen name for it. I think Kenny Killzone should set the tone nicely.

Sunday 10th November
Remembrance Sunday
Thinking of you, Grandad.

I had a dream last night.

Well, not so much a dream as a stomach churning nightmare that made me wake up screaming 'No! No! No! Not the custard creams!' at the top of my voice.

I was in the girls' toilets. There were pictures of pink cows all over the walls and the carpet was made out of furry pencil cases. I was strapped down in a dentist's chair. Mr Jones was leaning over me, dangling biscuits into my mouth with a pair of tweezers.

Out of the corner of my eye I could just make out his assistant. It was Norris. Well, Norris's head, arms and legs sticking out of a huge jar of peanut butter.

I'm never going to sleep again.

What made it worse was when my parents rushed in to see what the matter was. They'd just about managed to get me to calm down when Mum said she'd get me some milk *and a biscuit.*

I'm not sure the neighbours got much sleep after that either.

On the plus side, my cooking's getting better. My mashed potatoes actually tasted of potato, even if they weren't very mashed, and when I'd scraped off all the charcoal my sausages weren't too bad either.

Next time Dad says he's going to take the batteries out of the smoke alarm *before* I start.

Monday 11th November

Mr Jones has a big idea. He told us about it in assembly.

He glided in with a big black gown on. The rest of the staff followed behind him wearing the same gowns and the same smiles.

Once everyone was in, Mr Jones got straight to the point.

'Next week, Woodford School will have two days of Total School. This is one of my pioneering teaching techniques. I've used it for twenty-three of your Earth years. The way it works is that for forty-eight of your Earth hours everyone comes to school: pupils, teachers and parents. And, for those forty-eight hours, no one goes home!

'We will learn together and live together for two whole

days with no interference at all from the outside world.'
Mr Jones's eyes glinted. He had the look of a big purple
game hunter about to go on a shooting safari.

I felt like something about to get shot.

Mr Jones continued, 'As a result, your curriculum
from this week will see a few minor changes. Cooking
lessons will be compulsory as will first aid and lessons in
personal hygiene. The week will end with a giant feast,
and I have asked Miss Briars to accelerate her rehearsal
programme for the school play so that it will be ready
to perform on our final night together.'

Miss Briars looked delighted. But then so did everybody
else.

Permanently.

My cheek muscles were burning with the effort of
smiling but Mr Jones wasn't quite finished yet. He
dropped his voice so that it was almost a whisper.

'And just in case a certain ... journalist wonders about
contacting the press about my plans, he ought to know

that I've done it already. If he wants, I can show him the headlines in my office. They're rather good.'

What is it with head teachers taking my headlines?

Mr Jones spun on his heel and left with his gown swirling impressively behind him. He'd been practising.

It wasn't a great start to the week. It was about to get worse.

It was time to go to the girls' toilets.

The plan was to march in and get it over with as quickly as possible. It was a good plan and it worked well.

Right up until Norris and me got to the door.

At which point something deep within both of us screamed 'NOOOOOO!' at the top of its voice.

I told myself I was a fearless undercover reporter. I told myself I'd been in situations far more dangerous than this. Then I took a long, slow breath and put my trembling hand on the door. I stamped on Norris's foot and then he put his hand on the door as well.

Together we pushed and entered a world we were never meant to see.

We were alone. I resisted the urge to punch the air and shout 'Yes!' and ran straight into a toilet cubicle and locked the door. I sat on the toilet seat, Norris sat on the cistern.

Then we waited. Waited and hoped. Really, really hoped, that the next person to come in would be Justin Case and not someone actually going to the toilet.

Finally, we heard the door open.

Footsteps came our way. The person was in a rush, walking quickly and breathing heavily. They pulled open the cubicle door next to ours and fumbled desperately with the lock. It was either Justin Case or someone desperate for a poo.

There was a terrible silence. At any second I expected to hear a splash.

Eventually a weird, nervous voice said, 'Hello.'

I could have jumped for joy.

'Hi,' I replied, trying hard to sound like a girl. I think I tried too hard. When the echo died down there was more silence. I wasn't surprised.

'How are you?' I tried again, at about half the decibels.

'Fine,' replied the weird voice. 'Thanks,' it added after a bit.

As a conversation it wasn't going well. There was more awkward silence. Then Norris farted.

That got things started.

'Heh! What's going on? I thought we were coming here to talk!'

'It wasn't me,' I said, glaring at Norris who had gone

an interesting shade of pink.

'What do you mean it wasn't you? I just heard you.'

'It was my assistant.'

'Assistant!?' Justin Case's voice was rising higher and higher.

'Yes.'

'You've got an assistant to go to the toilet with you?'

'My assistant on the paper.'

'You've got an assistant for the toilet paper!? What sort of freak are you?'

'No! Not the toilet paper. What do you think I am? The *paper*. You know...'

'Oh, *that* paper.'

Justin Case calmed down a little. I went back to glaring at Norris.

'Yes, that paper.'

'Who is it then?'

'I can't tell you.'

'Why not?

'Because if we don't know who each other is then we can't grass on one another if we get caught.'

Justin Case thought about this for a moment.

'Okay, but why did they have to fart?'

'I don't know, it's a good question,' I said, still giving Norris the evils. 'I'll ask her. Why did you have to fart?'

Norris shook his head. The other day, when he was making points, I couldn't get him to stop talking. Now, all of a sudden, he'd gone off it. I wasn't going to let him off that easily.

'I'm sorry; I don't think Justin Case heard that!'

Norris's eyes widened in fear. He was going to have to try and speak like a girl.

'I'm sorry,' he said, in a voice that threatened to crack the mirrors above the sinks. 'I've just eaten a whole tin of baked beans. I lost control. I'm sorry,' he added again, the sweat pouring off him.

'It's alright,' Justin Case said after a long pause. 'I know what it's like. All I've eaten today are chocolate HobNobs and I'm going off them already. Let's just get down to business, shall we? What are we going to do?'

'We need to find out what Mr Jones is up to,' I replied. 'I don't like this Total School thing one little bit.'

'Me neither.'

'Problem is, I've already been following him loads. He's bound to put two and two together if I bump into him again. You need to do it for a bit.'

'Alright, I'll follow him,' agreed Justin Case. 'But you'll have to try and talk to Miss Briars.'

'Why would I want to do that?'

'Because she's the only other one who's not been affected.'

'But I just saw her looking totally spaced out in assembly, just like the rest of them.'

'She always looks like that.'

Justin Case had a point but he could tell I wasn't convinced.

'She's a really fussy eater you see. Only eats organic barley and vitamin tablets and weird stuff, so Mr Jones hasn't managed to get her to eat anything. We need everyone we can get.'

'Okay, I suppose,' I said, reluctantly. I'd rather talk to a brick wall than Miss Briars but these are desperate times. 'But what do I need to talk to her about? I mean, if she's not under his control why isn't she doing something about him already?'

'She hasn't done anything about it because she hasn't noticed.'

'Hasn't noticed! Hasn't noticed that the rest of the school has been turned into zombies? How can she not have noticed?'

'Because she's Miss Briars! Look, we have to let her know. No one's going to take us seriously but maybe they'll listen to an adult, even if it is Miss Briars.'

'Alright,' I sighed. 'But how do I get her attention?'

Justin Case didn't give an answer straight away. I got the feeling it was because I wasn't going to like it.

'You'll have to audition for the play,' he whispered.

Justin Case was right.

Mr Jones lied to us. I saw the Total School headlines at the newsagents. They're rubbish.

> ## TOTAL SCHOOL PLAN TO IMPROVE ATTITUDES AMONGST PUPILS AND PARENTS AT WOODFORD SCHOOL

Yawn.

> ## NO ONE'S TOO COOL FOR TOTAL SCHOOL

Trying way too hard.

> ## MR JONES READY TO TEACH US MORE LESSONS

Get a room.

I know a gatepost that could do better than that.

I've also discovered, beyond all possible doubt, that Miss Briars is totally mad.

In fact, all things considered, I don't feel I'm getting

the high standard of education I deserve at the moment. I auditioned for the school play, as agreed. The posters said it was going to be *Macbeth*. When I got down to the drama studio, I found out I was the only one who had turned up so Miss Briars wants me to play Macbeth. She's going to play Lady Macbeth. I said what about all the other characters.

She said she'd play them as well.

If I don't get horribly murdered by Mr Jones before next Friday, it looks like I'm going to die of embarrassment on stage instead.

I think Miss Briars told me a bit about the story but I tuned out after a couple of minutes. The drama studio is a weird room. It messes with your head.

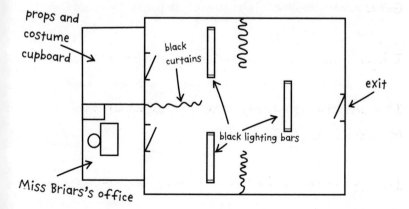

props and costume cupboard

black curtains

exit

black lighting bars

Miss Briars's office

It's about the size of two normal classrooms with four black walls and three black doors.

One leads to Miss Briars's office, one to the props and costume cupboard and one for the exit. On the ceiling are three black lighting bars with black lights on them and some black curtains to divide the room up.

I'm guessing Miss Briars likes black.

When she'd finished talking about Macbeth, I tried to bring the conversation round to the fact that the school has been taken over by a psychotic alien. Miss Briars said she valued my imagination but I needed to channel it into my character. I tried again and asked her if she'd noticed anything strange about the school recently. She thought about it and said that yes, now I came to mention it, she hadn't had anyone actually turn up for auditions before.

I'm supposed to learn my lines by tomorrow. There's about three thousand of them.

We had Food Technology this morning.

That means cooking.

Mr Frazer told us we'd be making hamburgers. He hauled three large sacks out of the food store cupboard and said they were full of all the finest ingredients we'd ever need. I thought they smelt like sweaty socks but everyone else thought they smelt great.

That's because their sense of smell has gone the same way as their brains.

We were split into pairs, given a recipe sheet and told to get on with it. Basically it involved putting a big spoonful from each sack into a bowl, adding some water and mixing it all up until it made a big grey blob. Then we took the big grey blob out, cut it into circles and fried it.

After that it smelt like fried sweaty socks.

For the pièce de résistance, we sliced open a bun, buttered it and stuck a burger in. I'd be lying if I said it looked like a hamburger. It looked like a big grey blob in a bun. Mr Frazer told us to eat them. Luckily I was with Lucy Hutch so I let her eat mine as well.

Norris sorted out another meeting with Justin Case after lunch. There was good and bad news.

The good news was that Justin Case said this time it was only fair to have it in the boys' toilets.

Justin Case said he'd been trying to keep track of Mr Jones but it was impossible. He said it was like he was everywhere. He said that, one time, he'd seen him turn a corner at the end of one corridor and ten seconds later he'd come walking up behind him from the other direction. I made a note of it for the survival guide.

And then there was the bad news.

Sally Coyle hasn't been in school for two days.

Sally Coyle has never missed school. She lives for it.

She's the sort of traitor who asks the teacher what the homework is *before* they set it. The sort of robot who doesn't have the imagination to leave school until the last club is finished. And the sort of person whose pencil case is better equipped than the average fire station.

The only thing that could keep Sally Coyle away from school is the sort of disease that needs lots of people in germ warfare suits to stop it wiping out most of the civilian population.

Justin Case said he'd try and get to the bottom of it.

I'm not sure he's going to like what he finds when he gets there.

Then it was my turn to tell Justin Case about Miss Briars. I told him she was a dangerous lunatic who shouldn't be left in charge of a glass of water, let alone a school play. I told him she had no idea what Mr Jones was up to and that trying to get through to her would be like trying to get sense out of Marmite.

Justin Case said I had to give it another go.

Then we talked about the hamburgers. Justin Case reckons they're not just for mind control. He doesn't know what else they're for but he doesn't like them. Norris thinks they looked quite tempting.

That's because all he's eaten this week is Branston Pickle.

We agreed to meet again tomorrow back in the girls' toilets.

Whoopee.

Thursday 14th November
Obesity Awareness Day
Bit ironic.

It didn't take long to work out what the hamburgers do.

I don't know what's in them, I don't *want* to know what's in them, but I do know that the whole school is now fat. Yesterday, Goran Sarta was a skinny Year Seven. Today, he looks like Mr Potato Head.

Before   After

And it's only going to get a whole lot worse. We got new timetables today. I don't know why they bothered. It's really easy to remember:

	Thursday
9 a.m. – 10 a.m.	Cooking
10 a.m. – 12 p.m.	Double Cooking
1 p.m. – 4 p.m.	Triple Cooking

You know what? I don't think Mr Jones wants to take over our minds.

I think Mr Jones wants to eat us.

As well as making you fat, the hamburgers have got another side effect: gas.

Both ends.

Walking from one classroom to another has become a major challenge. First, you have to negotiate the fat, wobbly zombies themselves. Then, you have to negotiate the gas cloud they move around in. I've walked into at least two doorways already and was choking so much at one stage that I nearly fell into the dustbin outside Art.

It would be great material for the paper.

If it wasn't for the fact that we're all going to die.

Luckily Norris had a brainwave and filled some bin liners with scrunched-up paper which we stuffed under our jumpers to make us look as fat as the others. We rustle a bit when we move but I don't think anyone's noticed.

The play rehearsal was the most embarrassing lunchtime of my life. We did the first bit where Macbeth meets the witches. Miss Briars said I had to try and look 'murderous' and 'confused' and 'vulnerable' all at the same time whilst she pretended to be all the witches. There's this line about the witches having beards, so she looked in the costume cupboard and found herself a different coloured beard for each witch.

If I don't get those images out of my head pretty soon I'm going to need some serious therapy when all this is over.

I was so traumatized I nearly didn't take on board some very important information.

Miss Briars is tooled up.

At the start of the play, Macbeth is supposed to be this super warrior dude. He comes on all caked in blood and fresh from the battlefield and stuff. So, Miss Briars got me a big shield and this massive sword to help me look the part. She said it was a genuine claymore. I asked how come she had one. She said that at weekends she did re-enactments of famous battles and had loads of old-fashioned weapons.

Result.

I told Norris and Justin Case about it later. I said that they should join the play and then we could have ourselves a little army. I'd like to see Mr Jones offer me a sweet with three feet of sharpened steel at his throat.

Justin Case was being really quiet. I asked him what he'd like to do to Mr Jones with a claymore. That's when he started crying like a girl.

I don't mean that just because he was crying he was like a girl. I mean he was crying and it sounded like a girl crying.

I thought I'd better give him a moment but Norris isn't into moments.

'Why are you crying like a girl?' he asked.

'Oh, that's typical,' Justin Case wailed in between sobs. 'You think that just because I start crying I sound like a girl.'

'No, it's not that,' Norris replied. 'It's your voice. You sound like a girl.'

'So do you, a bit.'

'That's because I *am* a girl.' Norris said, raising the pitch of his voice as far as it would go.

'Oh, please!' Justin Case snapped. 'If you're a girl then I'm Beyoncé! That's the worst impression of a girl I've ever heard. You sound like an elephant that's been sucking a helium balloon. And as for you, "Fiona Friend",' Justin Case continued, half crying, half shouting, 'don't think you're any better. I knew you were a boy before I even heard you!'

'How come?' I squealed - because I was still pretending to be a girl.

Obviously.

'Oh, come on! *The Woodford Word!* It's all one big ego trip, isn't it? We're running out of time here so let's stop messing about, shall we? I'm a girl and you're obviously boys. I mean, only boys could write notes that were *so* arrogant!'

'Well, only girls could whine so much!'

'Well, only boys could be so rude!'

'Well, only girls have to use three exclamation marks! And, anyway, if I'm such a bighead, why have you been so desperate to get my attention?'

'Because we need to stop him.'

Justin Case was starting to calm herself down again. Our deep and meaningful discussion had obviously helped clear the air. She blew her nose.

'So, get over yourself and listen,' Justin Case began, using her own voice clearly for the first time. I suppose it was sort of nice. 'He's got Sally, I'm sure of it. I was outside the Head's office and found a bit of paper scrunched up on the floor. It was ripped out of her planner. It said, "Help me".'

I let Justin Case's words sink in. It was almost impossible to believe.

'Sally Coyle ripped a page out of her planner?'

'It's worse than that,' Justin Case wailed.

'The handwriting was awful!'

Justin Case started sobbing again. I didn't blame her.

I wasn't happy about having a second person know who Jonny Jakes really was, especially as that person was now a girl, but it looked like I didn't have any other option. Our future was looking horribly clear. By the end of next week Mr Jones was going to eat all of us. And, if we didn't do anything about it, Sally Coyle was about to become the starter.

'Look,' I explained, after Justin Case had blown her nose for the millionth time, 'I don't want to know who you are and I certainly don't want you to know who I am, but, if we're going to rescue Sally, I guess we don't have a choice.'

'I won't tell anyone,' Justin Case promised.

'You'd better not.'

'Cross my heart and h-'

'Don't bother.'

'But–'

'Like you said, we need to get real, so let's just get on with it, shall we? I'll stand up on my toilet and then you stand up on yours.'

'What about him?' Justin Case asked, meaning Norris.

'If he stands up on the toilet he'll break it.'

'Oi!' protested Norris.

'Oh, belt up! Right, let's get this over with, shall we?'

'Okay then.'

'No stupid girly shrieking?'

'No shrieking.'

'You promise?'

'I promise.'

'Okay then.'

Slowly, we both stood up.

Justin Case shrieked. 'Oh my god it's–'

'What did I say about the shrieking! Why not just write my name on a piece of paper and give it to Mr Jones?'

'Sorry, I didn't mean to,' she apologized. 'I won't do it again. Okay?'

'Okay. Just make sure you don't.'

'Who is she then?' Norris asked, feeling a little left out.

'It's only Julie bloomin' Singh!' I shouted back down.

I can't remember exactly what Julie Singh said after that. Whatever it was, it was quite loud.

Mrs Singh, secretary/foghorn

Julie Singh, her daughter; overly sensitive

It's just gone midnight. Operation 'Midnight Rescue' is about to begin. Justin Case has just confirmed we're good to go and I'm waiting for a call from Black Panther (Norris said he wanted a code name as well).

If I don't get back, this is the end of my diary. The annoying thing is I know I'll come up with a much better last line than that in about ten minutes.

It's three a.m.

Operation 'Midnight Rescue' a success. Target identified and secured. Bogeys neutralized.

I'm not sure what that means. I just like saying it.

Five minutes before midnight we each crept out of our houses. We had black trousers and jumpers on, and Julie had given us tights to put over our faces. It sounded wrong but it looked right.

We met in the bushes by the school gate at midnight precisely. It was pitch black. We couldn't see a thing. Then Norris said maybe we should take the tights off until we got out of the bushes.

When we were sure no one was around, we rolled under the main gate and ran across the yard. At the front door, Julie got out the keys she'd stolen from her mum's handbag. There are some advantages to having the daughter of the head teacher's secretary join your investigation.

I shone my head torch at the door. As Julie put the key in the lock I could see the alarm code written on the back of her hand.

Julie looked at us. Once she'd opened the door there was no turning back.

We nodded and she turned the key.

The alarm started beeping. Julie opened the door and rushed inside.

That was the worst bit. Waiting for Julie to punch in the code with that horrible beeping sound getting faster all the time. I was sure somebody was going to hear it. I kept expecting police sirens to start wailing at any moment.

Then, finally, the beeping stopped.

We were in.

We tiptoed carefully along the corridor, keeping our head torches trained on the floor so that we moved along in three tiny pools of light. Without anybody in it, the school didn't feel like a school at all. It felt like walking around inside the belly of some giant sleeping beast.

As we got close to Mr Jones's office we slowed right down, pausing between every step to listen. It was deathly quiet. I half wished Mr Jones would just jump out and get it over with.

Julie gestured at Norris to take off his head torch and look through the keyhole. He bent down and put his eye to the door.

'Anything?' I whispered.

He stood up and shook his head.

Julie took hold of the door handle and twisted it as gently as she could. When it was fully turned, she pushed.

Nothing happened. The door was locked. Mr Jones obviously took his security a little more seriously than Mr Hardy had.

Julie brought out the bunch of keys again. Her hands were shaking and the keys started to jangle. Each little clink sounded like a cymbal crash in the deserted corridor. I held on to her wrist and the shaking got a little better.

Eventually she found the right one and turned it in the keyhole. The door creaked open slowly.

Mr Jones's study was empty. Or at least it was empty of Mr Jones, which was the main thing. We took the tights off our heads again and let out a long sigh.

We still didn't feel like speaking so we silently ran our torches over the room. It was unnaturally tidy. No documents marked 'Top Secret Plans for Taking Over the World' left out on the desk, no alien gadgets lying around and no sign whatsoever of Sally Coyle.

I was beginning to think that we'd wasted our time when I noticed my torchlight reflect off a dent in the steel cupboard. It wasn't much, but in a room that was otherwise perfect it stood out.

I nudged Julie and flickered my light over the spot to draw her attention to it. We walked over. I started tapping the outside of the cupboard and listening to the sound it made. I don't know why. It just felt like the sort of thing I should do.

Unsurprisingly it sounded like a cupboard.

Until it tapped back.

I tapped again. The cupboard did the same. Then it whispered 'don't scream!' in a terrified voice.

'Why not?' I asked it.

'Don't scream!' it said again.

'I wasn't going to!' I replied, a bit annoyed at getting nagged by a piece of furniture.

'Okay, sure, we promise we won't scream.' Julie whispered, nudging me out of the way and giving me a dirty look. 'Is that you, Sally? We've come to rescue you.'

'Yes, it's me,' Sally whispered through the cupboard door. 'Thank you so much for coming. Look, I'm sorry I keep saying it, but you mustn't scream. Put your hands over your mouths. Please.'

Julie motioned at us to cover our mouths.

'Okay, Sally, we're doing it,' Julie assured her. 'We won't scream, I promise. What do you want us to do next?'

'Have you got your hands over your mouths?'

'Yethhh,' Julie mumbled through her fingers. 'Whath shll we du nxt?'

'Okay, now you need to look up.'

We all looked up. We all screamed.

Luckily it sounded more like three goldfish celebrating a goal.

Four feet above our heads were two gigantic vampire bats. They were massive and were twirling upside down from the ceiling, fast asleep in their folded black wings.

But they weren't wings; they were teachers' gowns. And they weren't bats. They were Mr Jones

There were two of him.

'Can you see them?' Sally asked.

'Yeth,' we replied.

'Okay, you can take your hands away now. Disgusting, isn't it?'

I disagreed with Sally Coyle about many things but this wasn't going to be one of them. It wasn't as if Mr Jones wasn't weird enough without sleeping like a bat. To make it worse, gravity was pulling his features towards the floor. His stomach was sagging down to his chin and his massive nose was swinging below his head.

'I didn't think anyone would come,' she continued. 'I'm so grateful. You'll need to get the keys; they're clipped on to his belt.'

'Which one?' I whispered back.

'The belt round his waist, silly.'

'No, he means which him is the right him?' Julie asked.

'Oh, yes, I see what you mean. It took me a bit of time to tell them apart myself. He's the one with the slightly bigger nose.'

We looked up. Sure enough, the Mr Jones on the left did have a slightly bigger nose and we could just make out the silver tops of a set of keys under his cloak. I carefully moved a chair underneath him and got up on it.

'Who's the other one?' Norris wanted to know, while I tried to work out how I was going to unclip the keys. It didn't help that Mr Jones kept spinning all the time.

'That's Mrs Jones.' Sally replied, just as I was about to make a grab for the keys.

'Euuurrghhhh! That's gross!' Norris retched.

'I know, and when they kiss they make this sort of–'

'Too much information!' I whispered as loudly as I dared.

It was too loud. Mr Jones shuffled in his strange bed.

We waited, completely frozen, until he seemed to settle back to sleep. Pointedly I put my finger on my lips and glared at Norris.

The keys swung back into range. I held my breath and reached up.

I'd nearly got the keys clear of the belt when Mr Jones began to spin back again the other way. As I pulled the keys off, the clip caught very slightly on his trouser loop. It wasn't much but it switched the direction of his spin again.

Mr Jones's breathing changed and became shallower. We had to get a move on. I passed the keys to Norris.

'Which one?' he asked.

'Quickly!' I urged.

'It's a small one, I think it was gold,' Sally whispered. 'I can't really remember, you'll have to try them.'

As quickly as he could, Norris started trying out the keys. It wasn't quick enough. Mr Jones was waking up and so was his wife. They started mumbling and doing all those weird things you do just before you wake up.

'Come on!'

'I'm trying!' Norris moaned. 'Hang on, I don't think I've tried this one yet... Yes!'

Sure enough, the steel door swung open and there, tightly coiled, was Sally Coyle.

'Come on, let's run,' I said, hardly bothering to whisper any more. The mumbling was getting less mumbly all the time.

'We can't,' Julie answered. 'Look at her. She's been in there for hours, she can barely move.'

It was true; Sally was moving like someone coming out of a deep freeze.

Norris sprang to the rescue. He bent down and got his hands underneath Sally's knees and shoulders. Just as he'd scooped her up, a voice above us rang out.

'Who's there? What's going on? Brian? Is that you?'

Mrs Jones was rubbing her eyes.

'Brian! Someone's here. What have I told you about locking doors?'

'I did lock it!' Mr Jones replied groggily. 'What's going on?'

But, before they had a chance to find out, we had scrambled out of the door. I was halfway down the corridor when I realized Julie wasn't with us. I looked back to see her fiddling with the key in the lock. 'What are you doing?' I hissed.

'Locking the door,' she hissed back. As soon she'd done it, she snapped the key in the lock and ran after us. 'That should give us a little more time.'

We didn't bother closing the front door as we all pelted out across the playground. Norris was carrying Sally under his arm like a giant rugby ball. For once in her life she couldn't get out of school fast enough.

It was too dangerous for Sally to stay with Julie, so me and Norris had to fight over who didn't want her more.

She's at my house.

She's hiding under my bed. She keeps moaning that she's had enough of being curled up in dark, unpleasant places. I keep telling her to shut up and be grateful that at least I'm not going to eat her.

I gave her some of my Maths homework to keep her happy.

Back at school, Mr Jones has gone ballistic; anyone would think he'd had a bad night's sleep. In fact, the smiles have been wearing off everyone since they stopped eating sweets and started eating hamburgers. They're still under some sort of spell but now they've stopped looking so pleased about it.

As well as ripping open everyone's lockers, Mr Jones has got himself a pupil bodyguard. He doesn't go anywhere without ten giant hench-pupils around him. He's after me big time.

And if he works out who I am, he's going to suck my brains out through my ear with a straw.

He spent the whole morning going into classrooms, putting pupils into trances and trying to catch me out.

We were just at the eating stage of our lesson when he came into our room. He'd been working through the school methodically, from Sixth Form downwards, so I knew what was coming.

He put everyone in a trance straight away, including his bodyguards, and started wandering among us, sniffing and poking.

He'd almost got to me when I realized that, although the stuffed bin bags under the trousers and jumper were doing the job, my face was nowhere near as fat as it should be. I took a deep breath and puffed up my cheeks as far out as they would go.

Have you ever tried puffing up your cheeks for more than ten seconds?

It wrecks.

When he eventually came in front of me, I was doing my best to look like I was in a trance but I could feel myself growing redder and redder. The blood was pounding in my head and a bead of sweat began to trickle down my cheek. As he leaned towards me, spots of light started jumping about in front of my eyes and I could feel myself swaying. I was about to pass out when something terrible happened.

It came from Barry Devine's trousers.

It smelt like a vat of stale vomit and came with a rasp like the sound of splitting trousers.

There was a reason for that.

Mr Jones sniffed and turned his head. A purple cloud was puffing out of Barry's mangled trousers. Mr Jones smiled.

He made his way across the room to take a closer look and I finally got to breathe. Barry Devine had been pretty fat before the hamburgers came along; now he was a boy mountain. Mr Jones looked at his triple chin with satisfaction and prodded him like a piece of meat at the butchers. Then Mr Jones whistled.

In a few seconds, a large shadow fell across the
doorway. Mrs Jones had arrived.

She came over to her husband and they began to do this
weird circling around Barry Devine. They sort of dipped
and raised their heads at each other as they went round
and round. It reminded me of a pair of swans from a
film we'd seen about the courtship behaviour of birds in
Biology.

Apart from them not looking anything like swans.

The circling got quicker and quicker and the head
bobbing got more and more extreme. When it felt like
they couldn't go any faster, the Joneses stopped. Their
backs were arched, their necks stretched out and their
chins pointed straight up at the ceiling.

They stayed like that for several seconds, like toys whose batteries had suddenly run out. Then slowly they began to relax. Their necks relaxed back to their original position, their chins drew back in and together they left the room.

The pupils' trances lifted gradually.

Unfortunately, the air biscuit decided to stick around.

Even by the school's new standards of foul and unpleasant smells, this one took some beating. It lingered under the worktops; it swirled above the sinks and it swam straight up our nostrils.

For the first time, I wasn't the only one who'd gone right off hamburgers.

At lunchtime, me, Norris and Julie turned up to *Macbeth* rehearsals. Miss Briars almost melted with excitement.

'A cast!' she squealed with delight. 'A whole cast! You don't know how I've dreamed of a day like this! Don't go!'

she pleaded, as Norris decided that he didn't like having a teacher hold his hands and try to dance with him.

'I've got an idea for the start of the play, miss,' I said quickly, before Norris could get to the door. 'How about we have this big old battle scene, to show what Macbeth's been doing before he meets the witches? We could all do a slow motion fight; you know, swinging our swords around our heads and that.'

Miss Briars shut her eyes and tried to imagine what it would look like.

'Yes, yes. I can see it,' she said, swaying about. 'Macbeth appears through the mist, his sword flashing in the spotlight. Alongside him, his trusty comrade, Banquo, bludgeoning the foe with each mighty swoop of his mace...'

'Yeah! And Macbeth could actually have *two* swords, sort of like a double lightsabre,' I added.

'And I could be Macbeth's servant with a catapult *and* a dagger,' Julie suggested.

'And Banky-what's-his-name could have a big spear,' Norris joined in, suddenly much keener on drama than he had been a minute ago. 'And a proper shield.'

Between us we got her up to four swords, three shields, two spears, a mace, a dagger, a catapult and a pikestaff (whatever that was) before we thought we might be pushing it too far. We even managed to persuade her to let us take some of it home to practise with over the weekend.

If Health and Safety ever catch up with her, Miss Briars is going to be in big trouble.

Saturday 16th November
Inventor of the gas mask died 1966
We could so do with him right now.

Norris and Julie sneaked round this morning so we could all get the full story from Sally. We moved my bed against the door so my parents wouldn't be able to come in and surprise us.

Sally told us a lot we already knew: the trances, the sweets, the hamburgers. We asked her why she had been taken. She said that Mr Jones thought she was something to do with *The Woodford Word* because she was always writing stuff down. She said he searched all through her bag, but realized she was telling the truth when he saw that she was the only pupil he'd ever met who actually practised her spellings in the back of her books without being told to.

She told us more about Mrs Jones. Apparently she's been here the whole time. That's why Julie found it so hard to follow Mr Jones; half the time she'd been following his wife.

Norris asked what she thought they were going to do with her. Sally said she wasn't sure but they kept pouring this disgusting oil over her and tried to get her to eat some hamburgers. She refused to do it as studies have revealed that eating too much saturated fat reduces brain activity.

Unfortunately Sally hadn't worked out the whole 'we're going to get eaten' thing until Norris pointed it out.

Next time he tries to break bad news to someone, I'm going to have to push him for a four-minute warning.

Spent the afternoon on the survival guide. I've got the front page:

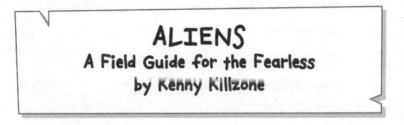

ALIENS
A Field Guide for the Fearless
by Kenny Killzone

And it's going to start with a few basic dos and don'ts.

1 <u>Don't</u> EVER accept food from an alien. It is their principal weapon. The food will either
   a) mess with your mind;
   b) turn you into a blob;
   or probably c) do both.

2 <u>Do</u> be on your guard at all times. They might be clever, they might even seem nice but remember, they just want to eat you.

3   <u>Don't</u> let the fact that they don't have teeth fool you. As far as I can tell, they've got at least two sets of lips, three tongues and saliva that could break down a horse (if in doubt, see 2).

4   <u>Do</u> carry a sick bag with you at all times. Whether it's their ability to suddenly rearrange their body mass so that certain bits bulge out unexpectedly, or the smell they make their victims produce, the fact is, sooner or later, they're going to make you puke.

Sunday 17th November
Dad's birthday
Oops.

Just when I thought I never wanted to go back to school again, my parents insisted on some 'quality family time'. I tried to protest but then my dad brought up the 'you didn't even bother to buy me a card' thing and guilt-tripped me into it.

So, we're going to spend the WHOLE of his birthday together.

Suddenly the thought of being eaten alive by Mr Jones doesn't seem like such a bad idea.

My parents are so excited about Total School. Apparently their school days were the best days of their lives.

I hate to think how bad their jobs are.

For some reason Mr Jones wants the parents to be in school uniform when they come to Total School, so we went into town on the world's worst shopping trip. Everywhere you looked, fat children were looking embarrassed as their parents tried to squeeze into white shirts, grey trousers and green jumpers.

If that wasn't bad enough, the uniform seemed to magically turn them all into naughty school children. Now I know why my dad's hair has all fallen out. If I had to tell them once that escalators should be treated with respect, I had to tell them a hundred times.

When we got back home it turned out the torture had just begun. They told me I had to pretend to be a teacher and teach them some of the stuff I've been learning this year. I told them it was rock hard and would go way over their heads. They said bring it on. So I did plate tectonics, square roots and sonnets.

I was right.

Worst of all, I had to watch them dance to the *School Disco* album they'd got. If there's a more terrible form of torture known to mankind than seeing your dad playing air guitar on the sofa while your mum pretends to sing into a hairbrush, I don't want to know about it.

Eventually I was allowed to go to my room.

Sally was trying to log on to my laptop.

'Hey! Get off! That's private!' I yelled.

'I wasn't doing anything,' she whined. 'I was bored. You can't expect me to just lie under your bed all day.'

'You got off easy. I've just had to spend the whole day with my parents, pretending to be back at school.'

Sally burst into tears.

It turns out that would have been her perfect day.

Luckily it wasn't too long before Norris and Julie came round for a planning meeting.

'Why are your mum and dad laughing so much?' Norris asked.

'I haven't managed to get a word of sense out of them all day,' I sighed. 'I'm not sure Mr Jones knows what he's letting himself in for.'

'What I don't get,' Julie said, 'is why, if he's planning on eating us, does he want our mums and dads there to watch?'

'Maybe he's planning on eating them too,' I said hopefully.

That set Sally off crying again.

'I was joking.'

'It's not very funny!'

'I think we've got to make our move as soon as possible,' Julie cut in, patting Sally on the back and trying to change the subject. 'The longer Mr Jones goes on, the stronger he'll get.'

'Sounds good,' Norris agreed.

'It's a good plan,' I said. 'Just remind me how we get Mr and Mrs Jones in the same place at the same time, avoid being splatted by their new bodyguards and create a big enough diversion so that we can catch them all by surprise?'

Julie told me to shut up if I couldn't be more constructive.

I told her to shut up if she couldn't stop being so stupid.

Then Norris decided to join in.

'Stop it! Just stop it!' Sally screamed.

We all stopped and stared at her. She had the pikestaff in her hand and was waving it around dangerously.

'I'm warning you!' Sally yelled, pointing the pointy bit of the pikestaff at each of us in turn. Her eyes were wild. 'I know nobody likes me! I know everyone thinks I'm just a goody-goody who isn't worth bothering with! But I've just about had enough! I may be a swot. But I'm a swot on the edge!'

'It's okay, Sally,' Julie said, putting her hands up. 'We don't think you're just a big swot at all, do we, boys?'

Me and Norris shook our heads.

'Erm, no, not at all. We think you're er ... you've er ... just got a giant brain,' I said, hoping I'd got the right sort of words in the right sort of order. 'Don't we, Norris?'

'That's right, we think you're great,' Norris said encouragingly.

It would have looked better if he wasn't still shaking his head.

Luckily Sally was starting to calm down.

'Arguing isn't going to get us anywhere,' she said, and this time I made sure our heads were all doing the right thing.

'Let's just keep thinking about it,' Julie agreed, carefully easing the pikestaff out of Sally's hands. 'We've got another rehearsal tomorrow lunchtime. Maybe we'll have thought of something by then.'

It's nearly midnight. I'm still thinking.

Monday 18th November

Thinking hurts. I'm trying a different approach.

I'm working on my alien survival guide and hoping I can give myself the answer by not trying to think about it too much - although it's two a.m., I haven't eaten all day and there's just a chance that I'm so tired I'm making no sense whatsoever.

Strengths

1   Five hearts. Hard to stop all of them at the same time.

2   Five eyes that can move around their faces giving them pretty much 360 degree vision.

3   They're annoyingly clever.

4   They've worked out how to control people's minds using food.

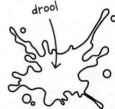

drool

5   Hmmm food.

6   I want some chips.

<u>Weaknesses:</u>

This bit hasn't been going so well.

Got it!!!

Julie was right. The longer we wait, the stronger Mr Jones gets. Everything's going his way and it's only a matter of time before he crushes us in his evil grasp.

I went back to racking my brains to think of something to give us an edge. So there's two of them. So they've got a whole bunch of bodyguards. So everyone is under their control. But surely Mr Jones has a weakness.

Then I finally realized what it was.

Mr Jones has never seen *Ninja Force 2*.

In particular he hasn't seen the bit where Ninja Force take out the two evil Japanese warlords, Masakuni and Yoshimoto, who have been holding the humble village of Fudai to ransom.

It's so simple.

All we have to do is: get hold of some minor explosives;
devise a plan for getting Mr and Mrs Jones into two
narrow gorges at the same time (corridors will do);
divide ourselves into pairs for a synchronized double
ambush and perfect the Leap of the Double-Backed
Tiger before dispatching the enemy with the razor-
sharp weapons we're whirling above our heads. By the
time we're done, Mr and Mrs Jones will have more holes
in them than cartoon cheese.

It's going to be awesome. I can't wait to tell the
others.

I wish it wasn't four in the morning.

I'd had about three seconds' sleep when Mum shook me
by the shoulder and told me I was late for school.

I said I'd only just got to sleep.

She said it was 8:30 and pulled my covers off.

She's like that on Mondays.

School was really weird in the morning. There were no special assemblies, no patrols, no inspections and, best of all, no cookery. It was like a normal day again. The teachers were normal too. I actually laughed at one of Mr King's jokes. It wasn't funny, it just felt good to be so bored again.

'Something's up,' Julie said, the moment we got to the drama studio.

'Yeah, but what?' I asked.

'I don't know but I don't like it. Haven't you noticed how quiet it's been? Oh, you can come out now, Sally,' she said, unzipping the huge hockey bag she'd been dragging behind her. 'Sorry about the socks but I thought the smell would put off anyone who got suspicious.'

Sally crawled out. She had her hand over her mouth and her nose was crinkled up. She wasn't having a good week.

I was just about to tell everyone my brilliant plan when Miss Briars appeared.

'Places, everyone! Places!' she shrieked. 'Right, I want to try the second witches scene! Come along, we've a lot to get through!'

It was time to break the bad news. I wasn't sure how she was going to take it but I couldn't take much more of Macbeth

'Erm, Miss Briars, there's something we really need to talk to you about.'

'This is not the time for arguing over artistic differences! We've got a show to put on!'

'It's not about the play, miss.'

'But what could possibly be more important than the play?' Miss Briars asked, genuinely shocked.

Norris decided it was time for some plain speaking. He was good at it.

'Miss, Mr Jones is an evil alien. We've got to stop him. He keeps putting everyone in a trance and he wants to eat us.'

Miss Briars opened her mouth to speak but shut it when she realized that, for once, she didn't have anything to say. She looked at us through her huge glasses as if she had only properly seen us for the first time. We all nodded.

She looked confused. She looked surprised. She looked like a drama teacher who'd just been told her boss was a dangerous, child-eating lunatic. She ran her hands along her necklace and twiddled the beads, deep in thought. Then something seemed to click into place.

'That *would* explain a lot,' she said.

'That's why we've come to the rehearsals,' Julie said. 'We wanted to tell an adult. He's tricked everyone else. They've all eaten some of his food. The sweets mess up your mind and the hamburgers turn you into a blob. You're the only one left.'

'So, you're not here for the smell of the greasepaint? The music of the bard doesn't sing to you?'

'Pardon, miss?' said Norris, who'd been enjoying the plain speaking.

'Oh, it's nothing. I just thought that perhaps, perhaps...' Her voice trailed off as she walked absently across to the props cupboard. She picked up one of the witches' wigs and spun it slowly on her fingers.

I was just wondering if we should have broken the news to her more gently when she turned back to face us. A new expression was on her face. Her eyes were sharp, her chin stuck out and her lips were thin. She almost looked like a proper teacher.

'Never mind! Never mind!' she yelled, her voice suddenly as hard and sharp as her face. 'You're right! This is a call to arms! This is no time for strutting and fretting our hour upon the stage. This is a time for action! We have things to do!'

She paused, her fist punching the air. 'What exactly are we going to do, by the way?'

'I'm glad you asked, miss,' I smiled. 'Hands up who's seen *Ninja Force 2!*'

Ten minutes later, we were ready to rehearse. Miss Briars had turned off the smoke alarm and got some theatrical smoke bombs ready to set off. I had taught everyone else the basics of the Leap of the Double-Backed Tiger. We were going to practise the ambush with sticks for swords and a speaker with a sheet over it to represent Mr Jones.

The first run-through wasn't great. The smoke got us confused. The speaker survived but it was a good job we'd only used sticks, otherwise Sally wouldn't have two ears any more.

By the third run though, things were looking a lot better.
We felt ready to try two attacks at the same time.
Mrs Jones was going to be a table stood up on its end.

I was about to give the signal to start when the door to
the drama studio opened.

'Ah, Drama Club,' said an all-too-familiar voice. 'I
thought so.'

Mr Jones smiled at his wife as they squeezed into the
studio with their many protectors. He wasn't handsome
at the best of times but being smug made him look even
more ugly.

'I told you it was the only one we hadn't checked, dear. How nice to see you all here. Hello again, Sally. And well done, Miss Briars!' Mr Jones clapped his weird hands sarcastically. 'I honestly didn't think you had it in you!'

Miss Briars's chin stuck out another inch.

'I do apologize for interrupting you in your work, I know how enthusiastic you are about the dramatic arts, but, as I'm sure you'll agree, there are some important issues we need to resolve. Oh, come now, please don't bother,' he said, as I made a half-hearted effort to pack some of the paper back under my jumper and pretend to go into a trance. 'I think it's time to stop playing games now, don't you? Our little game of chase is over. I've won.'

'In your dreams, fat face!' I yelled.

'Fat face? Is that the best you can do, *Jonny Jakes*?' Mr Jones chuckled. The bodyguards copied him. 'I thought you were meant to be good with words.'

'At least I don't have to brainwash everyone just to get a laugh, bogey breath!'

My insults were getting worse. They were, however, distracting Mr Jones from the fact that Miss Briars was edging her way over to the pile of weapons.

'Very good, very good,' Mr Jones clapped again. 'Your parents must be very proud. How are they, by the way? Are they looking forward to coming back to school? I'm so looking forward to having them all here.'

'You'll never get away with it!' I screamed.

It turns out that thinking you're about to die does nothing for your ability to say anything original.

Mr Jones lapped it up. In fact he was enjoying himself so much that he and Mrs Jones had forgotten to stay behind their bodyguards. They'd wandered, unprotected, into the middle of the room. They'd also forgotten to keep an eye on what the others were doing.

I looked at Norris. He was ready.

'Jonny, Jonny, I'm so disappointed in you,' Mr Jones crowed. Now Julie and Sally were ready. 'Haven't English lessons taught you anything? If you're not careful you'll be telling me that "the game is up" and "I'd better come quietly if I know what's good for me".'

Miss Briars looked like she'd been born ready. It had to be here. It had to be now.

I'd always dreamed of executing the Leap of the Double-Backed Tiger.

It was time to live the dream.

I shouted the Ninja Force attack command.

'Ninja Force, ready! Ninja Force, go!'

The girls darted into position. Miss Briars threw me my claymore and plunged the detonator. The room exploded with smoke.

Norris and I ran onto the girls' backs as Julie and Sally sprung upwards, growling and snarling at the same time. We somersaulted in perfect unison and were plunged dramatically into the swirling smoke, our weapons ready for action as we screamed out the Ninja Force battle cry.

I can't believe no one took a picture.

It was a great start and when I landed I was face-to-face with an astonished Mr Jones. Victory was mine. I drew back the claymore and was about to thrust forward when Norris's face suddenly appeared in front of me.

He'd got disorientated and instead of thrusting at Mrs Jones he was thrusting at me. Somehow I managed to dodge the vicious point of Norris's pikestaff and parried the enormous wooden shaft with my claymore, but by then the face of Mr Jones had vanished.

'Just get him!' I screamed, ignoring Norris's apology.

I spun out, slicing through the smoke with my heavy blade. At the end of its arc the sword hit something that felt a bit like a spacehopper and rebounded back the other way.

Norris thrust his pikestaff back in the direction he'd come from. It got stuck in something and he couldn't pull it out. There was a lot of whooping from somewhere behind me. Sally hadn't been set any

homework for a week and it sounded like she was
making Mrs Jones pay.

Then something barged into my right shoulder, knocking
my trusty sword out of my hand. In a flash I reached
down for the dagger strapped to my ankle and lashed
out at my assailant. After a few air shots the dagger
buried itself satisfyingly in a large roll of skin.

Unfortunately my hand followed it in.

With a huge effort and a massive squelch I managed
to pull free. My arm felt wet. I looked at it, expecting
it to be dripping with foul-smelling alien blood. It
wasn't. It was worse than that. It was dripping with
hot, salty, hamburger-smelling sweat. I doubled up,
retching and tried not to be sick on the claymore which
had thankfully reappeared at my feet.

By now the smoke was starting to thin. I knew we only had a few seconds of cover left so I swung the claymore wildly, backwards and forwards, where I'd last seen the surprised face of Mr Jones. There were some satisfying screams but still no blood as the sword just rebounded from one spacehopper-type thing to another.

Around me now I could see Miss Briars, Julie and Sally swiping and stabbing at the aliens in the last wisps of the smoke. Norris joined us, having finally retrieved his pikestaff, and by the end all five of us were in a perfect back-to-back circle of whirling steel. The bodies of our victims lay on the floor in front of us.

Sadly, as the smoke eventually cleared, we saw that none of them belonged to the right people.

Goran Sarta was crawling on his hands and knees trying to find the rest of his teeth. Peter Farrington and a load of others were clutching their stomachs and moaning. Sharon Stavely looked like she wasn't going to be able to play netball properly ever again.

The rest had a variety of minor flesh wounds and were trying to fall back to their protective positions around

Mr and Mrs Jones. It wasn't easy with the amount of sweat on the floor.

The Joneses didn't have a scratch on them.

'Bravo! Bravo! Encore! You know, I really didn't think the drama department could ever produce anything so entertaining. Oh, don't worry about them,' Mr Jones said, gesturing at his groaning bodyguards. 'There's plenty more of them. But I think I'd better have those now, don't you? Someone important might get hurt.'

Suddenly Mr Jones's head shrunk and his legs shrivelled. The spare flesh shot into his arms, which tripled in length, and he snatched our weapons before we'd even had a chance to work out what had happened.

It was like Mr Tickle.

From your worst nightmares.

By the time he'd rearranged himself back to his normal hideous self, Mr Jones's smile had vanished. Then he telescoped his neck so that his triangular mouth was suddenly warm and wet in my ear.

My ear wished it could move away as quickly.

'Do you know why I'm not going to eat you right now?' he whispered. Mr Jones paused to let me answer. I didn't feel like it.

'Because I don't like you.'

Mr Jones's neck drew back in. He clicked his fingers and two of the bodyguards pushed in a trolley loaded with cold and congealed hamburgers.

'If you don't feel like eating them now, don't worry,' Mr Jones said cheerfully. 'I'm going to give you the chance to build up an appetite. You never know, I may even want to see you again when you're a little less skinny.'

His mouth came over to my ear for one last pleasantry. 'Let's see you write about this one, Jonny Jakes.'

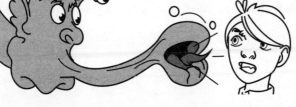

Then they left.

We heard them lock the door. Then we heard them board up the door. Then we heard them move lots of heavy things in front of the door.

Then all the lights went out.

You don't know what 'pitch black' is until you've been locked in a drama studio and someone's turned all the lights out. We were all too shocked to speak at first. Each one of us had just realized what complete and utter despair felt like.

It felt rubbish.

It wasn't long before the silence began to get to me. Every tiny sound was terrifying. I crouched down and started to run my hands over the floor around me. The more I felt nothing the more I panicked. Finally, my hand met another hand. I heaved a giant sigh of relief.

The two hands clung together. The other hand was

smaller than mine, more delicate.

'Julie?' I whispered.

'Cynthia,' Miss Briars replied, patting my hand. 'What warm paws you've got.'

For a few minutes pitch black suddenly didn't seem so bad.

I'd just managed to pull my hand away when a blue light lit up Norris's face. He'd remembered the mobile phone in his blazer. We were saved.

'No signal,' Norris sighed.

We were doomed.

At least the phone gave us something to look at. Norris held it up and started to shine its light around the room. The shadows from the stage lights and the lighting bars were weird and seemed to move by themselves, but the walls and ceiling looked depressingly solid.

'I don't suppose there's another way out of here, is

there?' Julie asked without conviction.

'I'm afraid not,' Miss Briars replied. 'But I suppose now is as good a time as any to sort out the props cupboard. Come on.'

Miss Briars crawled over to Norris, relieved him of his phone and then made her way to the drama office. There were a few thumps and other looking-for-something-type sounds. When she came out again, she was pushing a large box in front of her.

Most teachers have computers, textbooks and unwashed coffee cups in their office. Miss Briars has a secret stash of historical weapons and a big box of homemade scented candles.

It's a good job Miss Briars isn't most teachers.

Before we lit anything, we found a black curtain and taped it around the edges of the door. Mr Jones would have set guards outside and we didn't want them knowing we had light.

'What's this one supposed to be?' Norris gasped, as he lit the first one.

'Jasmine and tarragon,' Miss Briars informed us.

I'd never heard of jasmine and tarragon before but, as the smell invaded the room, I made a mental note not to set them alight if I ever came across them again.

In the flickering light we sorted the rest of the props into three piles: Useful, Possibly Useful and Rubbish. There wasn't much to go on the Useful Pile. Mr Jones had taken it all. There was a bow with no arrows, a catapult and two really rusty swords.

Norris got excited when he found a set of machine guns in a box. Miss Briars told him they were for something called *Bugsy Malone*. She said they were made from elastic bands and cardboard, and all they could fire was squirty cream.

Norris was still really excited until he found out they weren't loaded.

We'd got halfway through the cupboard when we

stopped for a break. As well as stinking the place out, the candles were hotter than I thought they'd be. I really needed a drink. Sally really needed something else.

That's when we remembered we didn't have a toilet.

Then we got on to remembering the other things we didn't have. Like food, electricity or any hope at all.

And the rest of the day sort of went downhill from there.

Might be Tuesday

My pen's running out. This will probably be the last thing I ever write.

I tried to sleep. I think some of the others tried too. But it's not easy when you're bladder's bulging like a beach ball.

When sleeping didn't work, I tried to sketch me and Norris doing the Leap of the Double-Backed Tiger.

I'm not sure I've captured Norris's best side.

Once you get used to the smell of the candles, another smell starts to creep into your nostrils: the smell of the hamburgers. They still smell disgusting - like a deep-fat fryer that hasn't been cleaned - but they also smell like food.

The moment I shut my eyes to try and sleep again, all I can see are hamburgers. Hamburgers piled high on a plate, hamburgers dancing with chips and drinking tomato sauce. If my mouth wasn't so dry I'd be dribbling.

This is depressing.

I'm going to stop now and concentrate on feeling sorry for myself.

I must have fallen asleep.

I woke up to the sound of the sky falling in. Or, as Julie put it, loads of fat kids all pounding on the floorboards above us.

'What's going on?' Sally asked, clutching her aching stomach.

'Killer turnips!' Norris screamed as he woke up suddenly. His dreams must have been even stranger than mine.

Miss Briars didn't say anything. I could just see her in the corner of the studio. She was sitting cross-legged, staring at nothing and making a low humming noise. Either she was trying to meditate or the last remnants of her sanity were finally giving up on her.

'I'm desperate!' Sally moaned, reminding all of us about the non-toilet situation.

'We've got to do something!' Julie whined, crossing her legs.

She was right and in that moment I realized that maybe Mr Hardy's assemblies hadn't been such a waste of time after all. If ever there was a time to 'dig deep', 'push the envelope' and 'show some character' it was now. Someone needed to take charge. 'Cometh the hour, cometh the man', that had been another one of his favourites. I didn't know what hour it was. Heh, I didn't know what day it was but I reckoned it was definitely time to cometh.

'Right, Norris, rip up the floor. If we're lucky, there might be some floorboards loose under the carpets; use a sword to lever them up if you have to. Sally, you check the walls, see if there's any gaps, weaknesses, anything! Julie, we're sorting out the rest of this props cupboard. We have to find something.'

It's amazing what fear, panic and really needing a wee can do. In two minutes the drama studio was a wreck, and me and Julie had completely emptied the props cupboard. But there was nothing else for the Useful Pile. We moved on to the office but it was just four stupid walls with stupid old posters of stupid old plays.

One of them was for *Macbeth* so I ripped it off.

'What's that?' Julie asked.

'Macbeth!' I shrieked in fury, ripping the paper to pieces. 'It won't leave me alone!'

'Not that. That!'

I looked up. Julie was pointing at where the poster used to be. There was a big square of wood where there should have been a brick wall.

I went for a sword. Between us, me and Julie managed to get it under the edge of the wood and tear it loose.

Behind it was a big black hole.

I brought a candle over for a closer look. Julie called the others.

When I put the candle into the hole it flickered on a stone wall opposite. There was nothing above but blackness. Looking down, I thought I could see the ground but I couldn't be sure. To the right were two thick cords.

Sally and Norris came in. 'You know what this is, don't you?' Sally gleamed, looking over my shoulder.

We didn't.

'It's a dumb waiter!' She explained.

It didn't help. She tried again.

'It's for lifting stuff up and down.'

That was better.

Sally reckons that before it became a drama studio, the room must have been some sort of food storeroom so the dumb waiter would have been used to transport food up to the kitchen.

She said dumbwaiters aren't called 'dumb' as in stupid; they're called 'dumb' as in silent.

This one wasn't.

As soon as Sally pulled on the cord, there was a horrible screeching, grating sound. Like someone playing a violin with a crowbar.

We froze and listened to the thuds on the floor above

us. They seemed to be carrying on as normal but we waited a few minutes until we spoke again just in case.

'We'll have to wait until they've gone,' Julie suggested.

'Or we could oil the bottom pulleys,' Norris said, leaning over the edge of the hole. 'I expect they're just down here. Have we got any oil?'

'Oh, sure. Hang on while I just pull out the emergency oil can I keep in my pocket for exactly this type of scenario.'

'I've got a chapstick,' Julie said, giving me the evils. 'It's not oil but it's greasy. It might work. Can you reach?'

Norris strained himself to reach as far over the edge of the hole as he could. It wasn't a good move for someone with a full bladder.

'Not without leaving a puddle,' he said, straightening back up and joining in with Julie on the evils. 'If only there was someone we could dangle into the darkness head first then we'd be alright.'

No one appreciates my humour.

Norris grabbed my legs as I walked my hands over the edge of the gap. He gradually lowered me down the lift shaft. My body shut out what little light there was, so I had to find the pulley by touch and rub the chapstick all over it.

Once I'd been yanked back up, we gave the cord another try. Norris pulled slowly. The screeching had all but disappeared.

As he pulled we could hear another sound. A rumbling. I looked up and saw the top of the hole getting lower. In a few moments a box was descending from above, filling the space where the hole used to be.

'Now, we just need a willing volunteer to test-drive it,' Sally said cheerfully. She turned and looked at me. Norris and Julie joined in.

I wasn't allowed to take a candle with me because Julie reckoned it would set fire to the waiter. Sally agreed and added she was pretty sure that, in such a confined space, I'd soon be overcome by the fumes from the candle.

Norris didn't think it mattered whether I took a candle or not because the cord was so old it was bound to snap before I got to the top, and I'd probably be dead from the fall anyway.

I gave Norris a gesture summing up how grateful I was for his concern.

If being locked in a drama studio without any light was scary, it was nothing compared to being pulled up in the dumb waiter.

In seconds, my world was totally black and silent. The candlelight and the whispers of the others disappeared. It was horrible. My head told me I was going up but my senses had nothing to prove it. I felt I was floating in a bottomless pit.

It was even more terrifying when I started to hear the creaking of the pulley at the top of the shaft. At any second I expected to plummet to my doom and my stomach somersaulted in anticipation.

By the time the waiter stopped going up I was curled into a ball of complete and utter terror.

I don't know how long I was like that. It might have been a few minutes. It might have been an hour. At last my survival instinct cut in. I had to stop myself panicking so I slapped myself.

Not easy in a confined space.

I told myself that if there was a way out of the lift at the bottom then there must be a way out at the top. I tapped the space in front of me. It was a wall. I started to panic again.

I forced myself to stop panicking and assess the situation. I was too coiled up to be sure but it seemed like there was light coming from somewhere. And, if there was, that somewhere must be the way out. I tapped backwards with my foot. Something wobbled and I let out a sigh of relief.

Another thing that involved a lot more effort than I'd expected.

Turning round was even harder and took me ages. But, when I was done, I could see a tiny sliver of light at the bottom of whatever was in front of me.

It was the most wonderful thing I've ever seen.

I put my fingers in the gap where the light was and lifted. Something started to roll up. I lifted it just enough to look underneath.

I was in the kitchen.

There didn't seem to be anyone around so I lifted the panel up a little further.

It was night. I could see the blackness through the tops of the windows. The light was coming from the fire exit signs. It was a thin and watery light but enough to see by. I lifted the rolling panel higher so I could crawl out. It felt good to be upright again. I gave the cord three tugs to let the others know they could come up.

It was freaky being in the kitchen. I'd sneaked around a lot of the school – it was part of the job – but I'd always been a bit scared of the kitchen. Or, rather, I'd always been a bit scared of the school dinner ladies.

They didn't like one of my stories:

THE WOODFORD WORD

THE SLOPPY GLOP MUST STOP

In another attack on our taste buds, the school kitchen has done it again. Following on from last week's rock-hard

My extreme close-up of a plate of congealed baked beans must have upset them. It upset everyone else. The whole school brought in packed lunches for the next week.

The kitchen was full of stainless steel doors and shiny

pans and knives. The fire exit light was weak, but with all the reflective surfaces it had a nasty habit of jumping out at you when you went round a corner. At the far end of the kitchen a large red door was slightly open and through it I saw a slice of heaven.

A toilet.

When I'd finished, I focused on my second priority: I needed food, I needed drink, but, before all that, I needed to find a new pen. That done, I filled a measuring jug with water from one of the sinks and drank it straight down.

My stomach was so empty I heard it hit the bottom.

I opened some cupboards to try and find some safe food. The first one was full of hamburger mix. So were the rest.

I was opening a fridge when a terrifying buzz zapped somewhere behind me. *FFZZZAAACK!*

Instinctively I fell flat on my stomach and squashed my nose on the floor.

I lay there trying to work out where the shot had come from. There had been no warning. The assassin was utterly silent. It was like being shot at by a shadow. I desperately wanted to sneeze but I held it back, knowing that, if I did, I'd be doing it for the last time. My attacker didn't strike me as the sort of person to miss twice.

I strained every fibre to hear a breath, a click, a footstep, something to give me an idea of where they were lying in wait.

Instead, I heard a giggle.

I looked around and saw Julie's head popping up out of the dumb waiter, laughing her head off at what I thought were my final moments.

That's girls for you.

'Heh,' she whispered. 'Over there.' She pointed across the other side of the kitchen. I turned to look and saw a neon circle behind a wire grille. There was some writing next to it. It read: INSECTECUTOR.

I'd just been attacked by an electric fly killer.

Once Norris and Sally were up, we continued our search for food. Nobody had managed to get any sense out of Miss Briars. Norris found a tin of baked beans that had fallen behind one of the stoves and hugged it to him. It was three years out of date but he was prepared to take the risk. Other than that it was all burgers.

Julie couldn't understand it.

'Why are there so many of them? I mean, everyone's massive already and they can't eat everyone all at once, can they?'

The question hung in the air like a dirty pair of pants. And, like a dirty pair of pants, no one wanted to really think about it.

Norris summed up everyone's feelings. 'Let's get out of here.'
The main kitchen door was locked. Norris gave it a shove to see if it was worth charging at but it wasn't going anywhere anytime soon. Julie tried out the fire exit but that didn't budge either. I could see that all the windows were meant to open at the top, but they were padlocked shut.

Plan A wasn't looking good.

'We could always smash them,' Norris suggested, pointing at the windows and picking up an extra large frying pan.

'Won't that make a big noise?' Sally said.

'So?'

'So, are you sure we want to draw attention to ourselves?'

'Of course we want to draw attention to ourselves,' I pointed out. 'In fact, I think we could do with some serious attention. I'm thinking police, fire brigade, rescue services generally. And I know just how to get it. You don't need to smash the windows, just one of these.'

I jabbed my elbow into the glass of the nearest fire alarm and waited for the sweet sound that would mean help was on its way.

Nothing happened.

I looked at the glass to check I'd broken it. Then I hit it again, just to make sure. There was a complete lack of ear-splitting noise.

Norris pointed out the reason. The cable that ran out of the fire alarm had been ripped out. I followed the trail of the ripped-out cable. It ended in a non-existent bell.

Just to add to the good news, Julie appeared out of Mrs Trumpit's office with her telephone. Or rather what was left of it.

'And the computer's the same,' she muttered.

'And my phone still can't get a signal,' Norris said, checking his mobile as it charged in one of the kitchen's sockets.

It looked like Mr Jones was making sure he didn't get any unexpected visitors.

We went back to the windows and looked out gloomily. In the distance there were lights on in the houses. Out there was electricity, TV and food that wouldn't kill you. It was all too much. I picked up the nearest saucepan and hurled it at the window with a primal scream.

Then everyone else started screaming.

That was because the saucepan hit an invisible force field and disintegrated in mid-air.

'Code Red,' screeched a piercing voice coming out of nowhere. Then it said it again and again and again.

'Time to go!' Julie commanded, heading for the dumb waiter. 'Ladies first, right, Sally?'

The girls started hauling themselves down as quickly as they could before Norris and I got a chance to change their minds. Norris called shotgun on the next go and pointed out that, being the biggest, he'd need the waiter to himself and I'd have to go last.

You find out who your friends are when it's Code Red.

I was taking some last minute-pictures of the fire bell for evidence when I heard footsteps outside. I rushed back over to the waiter and as soon as Norris got out I pulled like crazy to get the waiter back up in time.

A key started turning in the lock just as the waiter came up. Fortunately, the opening wasn't in direct view of the door so I still had a few seconds. I was curling up on the shelf again as the door opened.

With sweaty, shaky hands I tried to pull the panel door back down without making a sound. I still had four or five inches to go when a familiar voice bellowed 'stop!'

So I did.

'Listen,' Mr Jones whispered. 'I thought I heard something.'

I realized then that he hadn't been talking to me, but I had to try and close the last few inches before they got any closer. I tried to relax; one false squeak and we were all dead.

Millimetre by millimetre I slid the panel door down. When I couldn't see any more light, I stopped. But the danger hadn't passed. There was no way I could try and go back down with Mr Jones still snooping around. The dumb waiter still wasn't exactly quiet.

I waited and waited. I couldn't hear a thing, but with Mr Jones sneaking around and the panel door shut that was hardly surprising. A tiny draught came up from the bottom of the panel door.

I strained to hear the opening and closing of the kitchen door that would let me know I was on my own, but there wasn't a sound.

The tiny space was getting to me and I was finding it hard to breathe. I put my face close to the gap and sucked in the thin trickle of cold air, but it wasn't enough and everything went black.

JJ

I woke up with a horrible sinking feeling in the pit of my stomach.

The dumb waiter was going down.

Norris greeted me at the bottom. When I say 'greeted me', I mean he screamed at me and thrust a sword in my face. His eyes were wild.

'Norris, it's me,' I yelled, throwing my hands up to protect myself.

Norris brought a candle up to my face. I wished he hadn't. It smelt even worse than the other ones. When he was sure it really was me, his face relaxed a little and he lowered the sword. He was breathing unsteadily and looked completely exhausted.

He told me he thought I was dead.

I didn't quite know how to take it.

'Er, apparently not,' I tried. Hoping I wasn't.

'When no one tugged the cord we thought you must be dead,' he explained.

'Again, apparently not,' I replied.

'We thought Mr Jones would send someone down to trick us,' Norris continued. 'We thought he'd caught you.'

'Look, I get the idea but I'm okay! I'm still alive.' I breathed in and out exaggeratedly until it sunk in. 'I just couldn't pull the cord because they'd have heard you pulling me down. I was waiting for them to go, I think I fainted. Maybe I fell asleep. How long have I been up there?'

'No idea,' Norris mumbled. 'Phone went dead ages ago.'

Painfully I uncurled myself and climbed out of the dumb waiter. My legs were numb and it felt really weird to be upright. Norris helped me into the drama studio.

It was a grim scene.

Everyone was in their own little world of despair. Miss Briars had given up meditating and, without her glasses on, looked twenty years older. Sally was sitting with her back to the hamburgers and dribbling. Julie looked like she'd never slept her whole life. They smiled at me but

I could tell it took a huge effort.

I wondered again just how long I'd been asleep. How long my companions had been down here thinking I was dead and waiting for the final curtain.

Norris brought me over an old tin helmet. It was upside down with a spike at the bottom. He put it in front of me and made a scooping motion with his hand. He was so tired he'd lost the power of speech. Job done, he headed for a quiet corner to collapse into.

There was something lurking at the bottom of the helmet; something that smelt funny and had a thick red crust on.

'Miss Briars cooked the beans up over the candle. We left you some,' Julie explained. 'Sorry.'

When I tasted the beans I saw what she meant. These were not baked beans. These were baked beans with seriously weird stuff in. My tongue struggled to make sense of it.

'Raspberry Essence and Chilli Jam,' Miss Briars

informed me as the top of my head blew off.

As disgusting as Miss Briars had made them, the beans were still food and I forced some of them down.

'So what's the plan?' I asked in between mouthfuls, trying to sound enthusiastic. 'There is a plan, right?'

I looked around, everyone else looked away.

'Oh. I see.'

Even the baked beans couldn't hide the taste of defeat in the room. I tried to get rid of it with some helpful suggestions but none of them got beyond the 'we could try and...' stage before they found their own dark corner to collapse into.

All the party needed was the Grim Reaper to come and gatecrash. Instead, Mr Jones turned up.

As we heard the lockers being pulled away from the door, we half-heartedly forced ourselves to our feet and grabbed the remainder of Miss Briars's weapons. If Mr Jones was going to kill us, he was going to have to fight us first. It wouldn't be much of a fight but that wasn't the point.

It was almost worth seeing Mr Jones again for the look on his face, when he saw that we were neither fat nor dead. The same dark something I'd seen swimming at the back of his eyes during that assembly returned and his chest started heaving.

His bodyguards kept closely around him as he inspected the hamburger pile carefully. It was clear we hadn't touched it. He kicked the pile in frustration.

I couldn't take my eyes off his mouth. It was frothing with foul, acid-smelling dribble. I hadn't seen Mr Jones eat anything but sweets and biscuits since he'd  arrived, but now it looked like he and his three tongues were finally ready for dinner. I wondered what being licked to death would feel like.

It wasn't a clever thing to do.

With a deep breath, Mr Jones recovered himself. He looked at how weak and exhausted we were. It seemed to cheer him up.

He waved his new bodyguards into action with a flick of his wrist.

'Have fun, children.'

I charged at the nearest bodyguard, Kevin Hoyle, and swung a rusty sword towards the rolls of fat where I thought his neck must be. Kevin Hoyle stepped aside and swung his fist to exactly where he thought my chin was.

The others didn't even have the energy to get to the charge bit before they got smashed into a pulp.

As we lay groaning at his feet, Mr Jones started to walk between us.

'A shame, really,' he began. 'I haven't had an adversary with quite so much ... persistence for a long time. There was a troublemaker on Grar once who put up a bit of a fight, I remember. Of course, it made it all the more enjoyable when I crushed him.'

On the word 'crushed' Mr Jones made sure that his middle foot landed on my outstretched hand. It stayed there as he carried on.

'But "all good things come to an end". That's one of your Earth sayings, isn't it? We don't have that on Huurl. It loses a little bit in translation but our saying goes along the lines of "all powerful things will live for eternity by crushing the weak beneath them". Not as "punchy" as some of your headlines, perhaps, but I think you'll agree it grabs your attention.'

By carefully shifting the weight on his middle foot, Mr Jones was breaking my fingers. One by one. I bit my tongue to stop myself screaming.

'So, Jonny Jakes. We won't be seeing each other again. I shall miss our little chats but I'll just have to console myself with visions of your imminent demise. I'm afraid you won't be able to make our celebratory banquet, but I assure you your fellow pupils can't wait.

'And don't worry about your parents,' he goaded, heading for the door. 'They're particularly keen. They've loved being in school today. Especially the dinners. Funny, they haven't mentioned any of you.'

Mr Jones was about to leave. I looked around, desperate for one last chance to hurt him. The bodyguards had found the Useful Pile and taken it. The only thing within my reach was the spiked helmet.

I hurled it with my good hand at Mr Jones's grinning face. The helmet missed but a tiny splatter of beans sprayed his cheek.

There was a pause as Mr Jones's smallest and highest eye looked down and took in the tiny red stain.

He smiled and brushed the bean juice off.

Then he went crazy.

He started stomping up and down. His eyes watered and his cheeks puffed up. He was having some sort of allergic reaction.

He tried desperately to wipe the bean juice off his face and his fingers. Then his nose started to inflate. In seconds it looked like something that belonged on top of a steamship.

Then Mr Jones sneezed.

A huge ball of yellow-green goo flew across the room and squelched against the wall on the far side of the drama studio. Mr Jones screamed and held his head in agony. He wheeled on the spot like a demented demon.

So would you if you'd just sneezed some of your brains out.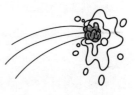

Clutching his head, Mr Jones staggered towards the door. I ran over and tried to scoop some more of the baked beans out of the helmet, but there was nothing left other than flaky crumbs that just stuck to my fingers.

As Mr Jones left, he waved a hand at the various water pipes running along the bottom of the room.

'Rip them off,' he commanded his bodyguards. 'All of them!' he screamed.

Then he was gone.

The bodyguards didn't waste time in kicking the pipes apart and away from the walls. I hadn't realized just how much water was running through the drama studio until it all started pouring out. It was a big room but within seconds we were sloshing around in an inch of water. To make matters worse, we could hear a lot of noise in the corridor.

A lot of 'bricking-up-the-door-so-everyone-in-the-studio-drowns' sort of noise.

There was no time to talk about what we'd just seen. We headed straight for the dumb waiter and whatever waited above us.

Sally and Julie squashed in again first and were about to go up when Miss Briars thought of something.

'Take these,' she said, handing over some of the Tupperware boxes me and Julie had cleared out of her office. 'Turmeric, Pineapple and Paprika Paste; Cracked Black Pepper and Cinnamon Mix; and Nutmeg, Celery and Marmite Surprise. If there's any one up there, fire at will.'

As soon as they went, Miss Briars sploshed back for more highly flavoured ammunition. I made sure my notebook stayed dry and tried not to think about the pain flooding up my forearm.

When we got the three tugs on the cord, Norris let me go next. I wasn't going to be much good at pulling with only one working hand.

'It's all clear for the moment,' Sally reassured me when I got up, then she went back to help yank on the cord.

It was night-time in the kitchen again and there was no sign of life.

Miss Briars was last up. She was wet to the waist but her top half was covered in dust. She had a large yellow box with her. The box had a big red cross and various warning stickers on it. Most of them said DANGER.

We waited for an explanation.

'I've been saving it for a special occasion,' Miss Briars said cheerfully.

When we'd had a chance to go to the toilet and gulp down some water, we huddled down and whispered as quietly as we could.

'So, what just happened down there?' Norris asked. It was a good question.

We established three key points:

1   Mr Jones doesn't like Miss Briars's cooking.

2   Our friends and family are all going to be eaten tomorrow.

3   Mr Jones hasn't realized we can get into the kitchen.

'I get it!' said Sally, as if she'd just worked something out. 'The hamburgers! He's more sensitive to things than we are.'

'I hardly think trying to eat everybody is being sensitive,' Miss Briars argued.

'No. Not sensitive like that, miss. Sensitive to strong flavours. That's why he's been feeding everyone those bland hamburgers. They make you fat but maybe they tenderize you at the same time.

'He's sensitive to light as well,' I said, thinking aloud. 'Remember that time we first saw him?' Norris nodded. 'He never goes outside without something protecting him from the sun.'

'So, we need to throw more food at him?' Norris rounded up. 'Especially if it's spicy, herby and weird like miss's. No offence, miss.'

'None taken,' Miss Briars replied. 'I suggest we spike the hamburger mix and work on ways of propelling it at Mr and Mrs Jones.'

'What about the ... that?' Julie pointed at Miss Briars's big yellow box.

'All in good time,' Miss Briars purred as she gave it a stroke.

We split up. Miss Briars and the girls started mixing extreme flavours into the hamburger mix. Norris and I started thinking about how to fire it.

The obvious thing was just to get a load of long-handled serving spoons and flick little balls of it. Norris wanted something a bit more spectacular though. I asked him what he was going to do with a bunch of cooking stuff and some cutlery. He said he wasn't quite sure yet but he had a name already worked out: The Spatulator.

I left him to it and went to see if I could find any ice for my fingers.

I found some in the bottom of a freezer. It was like a bubble pack of ice cubes and I wrapped it in a tea towel around my throbbing hand.

I explored some more. In the furthest row of the kitchen, between the shelves with the tea towels and tablecloths and the row of industrial-sized microwaves, there were loads of trolleys. They were parked in a long line and covered in crisp white cloths. They hadn't been there last time. I reckoned they were going to be used to ferry stuff to the banquet.

I'd found a way out of the kitchen.

One of the trolleys had a cake with 'WELCOME'
written on it in curly, icing-sugar letters. I could smell
cream, sponge and jam. The last thing I ate was so
disgusting it made Mr Jones's head explode and now,
here I was, in front of a gorgeous-smelling cake that
I knew I couldn't eat.

I did the only thing I could do.

I drooled.

'Over here,' I whispered to the others as loudly as I
dared. 'Mind the puddle.'

Everyone came to stare at the cake. It was enormous.

Miss Briars was rubbing her hands in glee.

'What's up, miss?' Norris asked.

'I think I've just found "something special",' she
smiled. She locked her fingers together and stretched
them out in front of her like someone about to break

open a safe. 'Bring me my box.'

As Norris and Miss Briars worked on their weapons of mass destruction, the rest of us got on with the hamburger mix.

There were three main jobs: Sally took the existing patties out of the fridge, put them into a mixing bowl and added some of Miss Briars's flavouring before forming them again, slightly smaller. Julie was making ready-to-throw burger balls with the leftovers.

I supervised.

'Are you just going to stand there?' Julie asked, as I wondered how the school was going to take to having their hamburgers spiked. I reckoned they were going to freak out.

'I've got a bad hand.'

'That still leaves your other hand. You could stir some of this into the sacks.' She handed me a box of Rosemary and Fennel Fusion.

'I'm disabled. I'll never be able to clap hands again.'

'Not if you don't help out, you won't.'

I took the hint and started pulling out three sacks of the dry hamburger mix from a cupboard. I poured Rosemary and Fennel Fusion into each sack and stirred it in with a long wooden spoon.

I'd got through three more tubs of herbs when I got to the final cupboard on the row.

'Huh, this one's locked,' I said, pointing it out to the others. 'Which, now I come to think of it, is really weird, because it doesn't actually have a lock on it.'

'It's glued,' Norris said, looking closely. 'I'll get a knife.'

With a bit of persuasion, the glue around the cupboard door eventually gave up and Norris yanked it open.

The smell hit us.

It wasn't a bad smell, it was just powerful. Like someone had lifted the lid off a thousand spice bottles all at the same time.

We'd found where Mr Jones had hidden all the flavour.

There was puree, there was paste, there were cubes and cartons. Mr Jones wouldn't know what had hit him.

It was a long night but, by the time we'd finished, we were armed to the teeth. Sally and Julie had spiked thousands of burgers and moulded hundreds of burger balls packed with just about every flavour known to mankind. I'd made sure that any other fresh burgers made from the sacks of dry mix would be equally horrible. Norris had perfected The Spatulator, and Miss Briars had rigged up the cake so that one of the candles acted as a fuse for *The Big One*.

She explained that it was the ultimate in theatrical explosions and required a special licence.

Norris asked if he could apply for one.

She also pointed out that, in addition to the force of the explosion, anyone near the cake at the time would be exposed to an extreme dose of curry powder.

When the first fingers of light showed in the sky outside, we tidied up. We rearranged the trolleys so that five of them had space on their bottom shelves for us. Then we each took a pile of Julie and Sally's spicy burger balls, stuffed our pockets with anything else we might be able to throw, squeeze or squirt at our enemy, and tried to make ourselves comfortable on the trolleys.

There's nothing left to do but hope we don't get discovered and try to get some sleep.

It didn't happen.

Half an hour later the kitchen was throbbing with noise. It seemed like the whole school was in there with us. When the burgers hit the frying pans the smell was tremendous.

The trolleys shook all day long as fat footsteps pounded

up and down. The trolleys vibrated so much we had to hug our weapons to our chests to stop them jumping out onto the floor.

It would have been easier to sleep in a washing machine.

It was agony trying to keep within the four white walls of the trolleys. My neck and shoulders felt like someone had tied knots in them. I must have tried hundreds of slightly different positions but I couldn't get comfortable for a second. I'd always found having pins and needles quite funny before but it's a pretty sick joke when it feels like your arm's going to fall off.

Even worse was not having the faintest idea what was going on. Although there were loads of people in and out of the kitchen, not one of them said a word. There was just the thumping of feet, the clanging of pans and the sizzling and spitting of frying burgers.

At some point during the day I heard at least one trolley being wheeled away. My whole body broke out into goose pimples thinking we were about to be found out.

I tried to work on my Alien Survival Guide to take my

mind off it all. It was good to finally have something to put in the Weaknesses section.

Alien Weaknesses:

1 Sensitive to direct sunlight and any sort of criticism.
2 Have an allergic reaction to strong flavours and spicy food. Have been known to sneeze their own brains out.

However, by the time my trolley finally started moving I'd gone into some sort of trance. I was so tired and giddy I was starting to see things in the folds of the cloth. It had got to the stage where the little people had started talking to me.

If I had stayed in the kitchen any longer I'd have started talking back.

The person pushing my trolley was grunting with the effort. I just hoped they didn't start looking underneath to see why it was so heavy.

As the adrenalin kicked in, the fuzziness started to wear

off. My hearing became hypersensitive. I strained for the sound of other trolleys. I could hear two sets of squeaking wheels quite close to me and wondered who might be on them.

It wasn't hard working out when we'd got to the main hall. If the squelch and suck of bucketfuls of saliva hadn't given it away, then the gulp and swallow of hundreds of mouthfuls of half-chewed food cleared things up.

And still no one talked. Or, if they did, they did it with their mouths so crammed full of hamburger it was impossible to make out a word they were saying.

The tension became unbearable.

The plan was to wait until Mr Jones had lit the candles on the cake. Once *The Big One* had done its worst, we'd burst out of our hiding places to finish off any parts of Mr and Mrs Jones that were left. After that we'd have to see what sort of mood their minions were in.
It was a simple enough plan, but behind my cloth I didn't have the faintest idea what was going on and it was driving me crazy.

My ears started playing tricks on me. Every sound started to sound like Norris or Julie breaking cover or giving some sort of signal to attack. Then the voices started. One voice in my head told me to attack. Another voice told me to sit tight. A third voice asked me if I wanted cream with my muffins.

I told the little people they weren't helping.

I had to look.

My trolley had been unloaded the minute it had arrived in the hall and it hadn't moved since. I was sure everyone would be far too busy eating to notice me. All the same, I lifted the cloth up very carefully.

It was a relief to see a world beyond the tablecloth. Even if that world was full of people gorging themselves on the hamburgers from Huurl. The hall was lit by candles. They cast large, sinister shadows on the walls but at least these ones didn't smell.

On every table the scene was the same. In the centre of each table was a rapidly disappearing mountain of burgers and around the edge were rapidly expanding mountains of pupils and parents. Their table manners had disappeared along with everything else and everyone ate, caveman style, with greasy, greedy fingers.

I looked around for my parents. I couldn't see them anywhere. For a moment I thought that somehow they had escaped. Then I realized I needed to be looking for much fatter versions of my parents. That's when I saw them and my stomach lurched.

They were as fat and vacant and doomed as everyone else. If anything my dad was fatter.

On the stage was a table with a red and gold velvet tablecloth, presumably for the head teacher and his hideous wife, but there was no sign of them yet. In front of the table was one of the catering trolleys. I could tell by the cake-like swelling beneath the cloth which one it was.

I stuck my head back under the cloth and waited.

I'd completely forgotten we'd spiked the hamburgers until I started hearing the screams.

Actually 'screams' doesn't really do them justice, they were more like something you'd hear if you tried to boil an elephant in a pressure cooker.

I had to take another look.

A hall full of red-faced diners were clutching their stomachs and throats in pain. The spiked burgers had finally reawakened their taste buds but their mangled brains were still telling them to eat. Their eyes were bulging out beyond their doughnut cheeks.

No one was in any state to notice me, so I took the risk of looking out the other side of the trolley. The scene was the same. I saw a twitch in the cloth of a trolley across the hall. I couldn't see who it was but I knew what they were thinking.

Where were the Joneses?

The piles of hamburgers were growing smaller and smaller. Some tables had almost exhausted their supply. The wailing and screeching had reached some sort of peak and was beginning to fade into gentle moaning.

Everyone was enormous.

No one showed any signs of leaving their tables but, if they had, I don't think they would have made it. People were literally wedged fast in their chairs, their enormous swollen stomachs heaving against the edges of the tables.

Gradually a silence descended on the room. The candlelight flickered but it was about the only thing that moved.

'Good evening, everyone.'

Mr Jones's mocking voice boomed suddenly out of hidden speakers. If evil had a sound, this was it.

The hairs on the back of my neck stood up. The hairs on the back of everything stood up.

'I trust you've all eaten well,' Mr Jones continued. I looked around to see if I could see him, but I guessed he was hiding somewhere whilst his dinner fattened itself up.

'Thank you all for coming. Forgive me for not joining you for the first course but I needed to build up my appetite for the main event. You see, this really is a special occasion. Not just for Woodford School but for my family. You haven't met my family, have you?'

Mr Jones was playing with his food.

'Well then, let's get acquainted. Ladies and gentlemen, boys and girls, please welcome my eldest son, Hoorraarg.'

A smattering of soggy applause rippled feebly across the room. I looked behind me and saw another complete copy of Mr Jones take a place at one of the tables. The man on his right attempted to lift his head and smile a welcome, but it was a step too far and his cheek crashed back on the table.

Mr Jones continued. 'And how about a warm reception for my eldest daughter, Sherraall?'

One by one, each of Mr Jones's seventy-three children appeared and occupied the spare seat that had been left at each of the seventy-three tables. The children all looked exactly the same. By the time the youngest daughter took her seat, no one was in any fit state to be doing any clapping. In fact most of the room was asleep.

'Children, welcome. It's wonderful to see you.' Mr Jones's voice was now full of affection. 'Your mother's right, we really should do this more often. You know what she says, "a galaxy is full of stars but nothing's home until it's ours".'

The children chuckled politely. My blood ran cold.

'Now then, children, as usual your mother's been working on a version of a local delicacy to accompany your first meal here. I need hardly remind you about the effort your mother puts into these sort of things, so just you make sure you show your appreciation. My darling slotherings, we give you ... cake!'

I remember clearly the chanting: 'Cake! Cake! Cake!'

I remember clearly my horror as the Jones children pulled their vicious looking cutlery out of their chin sacks and started bashing it on the table in unison.

And I remember clearly my whole body turning to ice when, just as Mr and Mrs Jones took triumphantly to the stage, I saw Julie's face peering out beneath the cloth of the trolley with the cake on.

After that, everything's a bit of a blur.

Time stayed still as Mr Jones struck a match and brought it to the first candle on the cake. I could see Miss Briars's eager face poking out of the trolley across the hall from me. She couldn't see me and I could tell she hadn't spotted Julie. Julie couldn't see me either.

She had no idea the cake had been moved to her trolley.

As the candle flared I forced myself back to life. I clattered out of the trolley and started waving my hands and screaming like a madman. Seventy-three alien offspring wondered what the heck sort of entertainment their parents had booked for the family reunion.

'Julie! Get out! The cake! It's just above you!'

Julie's face fell in horror and she tried desperately to get out of the trolley, but her body had seized up. She half stumbled, half fell out of the trolley and tried to pull herself away with her arms.

She was about two metres away from the cake when it exploded.

I don't know why Miss Briars thought she might need a special effect that could take out a small village but *The Big One* lived up to its name.

It wasn't just the cake that exploded. Mrs Jones, who had been standing right over it with a large knife, was blown apart and the whole hall was instantly coated in marzipan, icing sugar and luminous alien guts. It brightened the place up.

In the smoke, where the cake and Mrs Jones had once been, there was no sign of Mr Jones or Julie. Unlike his wife, Mr Jones had realized that something was wrong with the trolley and had ducked down to investigate.

The blast woke everyone up. Whether it was because of the sheer force of the blast, or the death of one of their torturers, it wasn't clear, but the pupils and parents looked different straight away. Their eyes had lost that glazed-over look. They were staring at themselves and pinching the huge rolls of flab on their arms. You could see them wondering how it got there.

Mr Jones's children were also staring and pinching themselves. But that was because their mum had just been vaporized.

Suddenly a hail of grey balls filled the hall. Norris had lifted the cloth off his trolley and unleashed The Spatulator. The spicy meatballs had the same effect on Mr Jones's children as they had had on him and the room soon rang with the sound of painful alien sneezes.

Miss Briars and Sally had also broken cover and were letting rip with long-handled spoons.

I couldn't move. I just kept staring at the spot where I'd last seen Julie.

'Watch out!'

Norris's warning jerked me into what was left of the real world. I turned my head and saw a group of Joneses heading my way. They'd taken advantage of Norris having to reload and had already cut off my route back to my trolley.

'You're going to pay for what you did to our mother, earthling!' The largest of them snarled and shot his arm towards my throat.

A clammy hand lifted me off the ground and squeezed. My brain screamed for oxygen. My arms flapped uselessly at the alien's thick purple hide. Jones junior laughed. I couldn't tell if it was for effect or if I was tickling him.

I gave up struggling. A part of me knew this was always how it was going to end.

As my right arm fell limply back down it brushed against my trouser pocket.

My trouser pocket full of tomato puree.

On reflection, it was probably a good job that my brain was beginning to shut down. If it hadn't, it might have stopped me squeezing the tube of puree with my broken hand. It hurt. It really hurt. But it didn't hurt me as much as a tube of tomato puree in the face hurt my attacker.

In a hall full of screaming people, the scream was still loud enough for everyone to turn and look. Mind you, they turned away again pretty quickly.

That's because brain juice was spraying their way.

Norris soon put paid to the rest of the mob once he'd reloaded The Spatulator, so I went back to looking for Julie.

The smoke around the stage was finally clearing.

I could make out the trolley that the cake had stood on. It was scorched but still standing. Looking up I could see, by a huge hole in the ceiling, that the force of the explosion had gone mainly upwards.

There was a chance Julie had made it.

I called her name again and again. Eventually I got a reply.

'Hggggffffuuummmpph.'

I moved toward the sound of her muffled voice.

'Julie, I'm here. What's the matter?' I asked.

Julie didn't reply. I realized why when I saw Mr Jones emerging from behind one of the hall's scabby blue curtains. It's hard to reply when your face is stuck under the leathery arm of an alien scumbag.

Mr Jones looked different.

He had a chair leg through his knee.

We stared at each other, each of us weighing up our next move.
I had a deadly meatball in my hand. He had Julie.

'Persistent enough for you?' I asked.

'Don't think I won't,' Mr Jones replied, opening his mouth and pushing Julie towards it. 'She may be tough and tasteless but I'll still do it. Put the meatball down and you might just get your girlfriend back.'

'Put her down and I might just let you walk away,' I replied.

I was trying to be cool but it wasn't very convincing. I was shaking all over.

He'd just called Julie my girlfriend.

Julie caught my eye. I tried to make a gesture to show her that all this talk of girlfriends had nothing to do with me. She made a gesture that showed me that she had a tube of garlic paste in her pocket and I needed to keep Mr Jones talking.

'So ... er...' I tried.

But Mr Jones wasn't in the mood for small talk. Miss Briars, Sally and Norris were laying waste to the remainder of his children, and he was in the mood for revenge.

'Put down the meatball or I'll eat her. I'll count to three. One, two...'

My brain froze. My mouth flapped uselessly up and

down. Now that someone's life depended on it, I couldn't think of a thing to say.

So I started singing.

Mr Jones stopped counting. In fact, after a few seconds the whole room stopped what they were doing.

It was that bad.

I don't know why but the first song
that had come into my head was 'Twinkle Twinkle Little Star'. It was so pathetic Mr Jones couldn't resist flinging his head back for a final victorious laugh.

It was a bad move.

In one swift movement, Julie grabbed the tube of garlic paste, twisted off the cap and sprayed it straight into Mr Jones's gaping jaws.

I stopped singing and there was a silence as all eyes turned to Mr Jones.

For a second or two, nothing happened. Then it didn't happen for another couple of seconds. Mr Jones swallowed with a bemused look on his face. To everyone's surprise it looked like the danger had passed.

Then Mr Jones blew up.

I felt truly sorry for the cleaners.

I rushed over to where Julie lay in a crumpled heap.

She was covered in a thick, sticky coating of foul-smelling gunk. I pulled her to her feet and asked her if she was okay. She said that apart from needing to spend the whole of next year in a bath she was fine.

Amongst the gore and the smoke and the smell of a thousand spice racks, I saw Norris, Sally and Miss Briars coming over to join us. The last of the Jones children had been taken care of, courtesy of a well-aimed pot of garam masala.

We looked at each other. We looked at the scene of devastation around us.

Then we headed for the exit.

I stopped at the payphone by the main entrance and dialled nine-nine-nine.

The operator wanted to know which emergency service I required. I didn't know where to start.

'Just send them all down to Woodford School,' I said.

'But I need you to tell me the nature of the incident,' the operator complained.

'Trust me. You wouldn't believe me if I did.'

'At least tell me your name, please.'

'I don't think so. I've done way too much of that recently.'

'But sir...' the operator started whining.

'Listen, just get everyone here now! I've got a deadline to meet and this time I'm not going to miss it. If you really want to find out what happened, you'll have to do the same as everyone else tomorrow morning.'

'What's that, sir?'

'Get a paper.'

THE WOODFORD WORD

WORLD EXCLUSIVE
SPICE KNOWING YOU

Last night the world said goodbye to some unwanted visitors in the biggest food fight ever recorded

EXCLUSIVE INTERVIEW

NAME:
Malcolm Judge

PROFESSION:
Author and teacher

BIO:
Malcolm Judge is a drama teacher in Cumbria. He enjoys cycling, skiing and making stuff up. He invented Jonny Jakes so he could be rude and get away with it.

Describe your book in one sentence.

Jonny Jakes offends pretty much everyone but, on the plus side, he does save the world from an evil alien.

Would you have joined Jonny's resistance group or would you not have been able to resist the sweets…?

I'm not good at saying no to sweets.

Do you think any of your teachers were secretly aliens?

No. Aliens would have had better clothes.

What was your favourite book as a child?

The Hobbit by J.R.R. Tolkien. I've always loved adventure stories and the success of the underdog. As a young adult, my favourite book was *Catch-22* by Joseph Heller. It was mad, bad and I couldn't put it down.

What is your favourite book now?

The Adventures of Huckleberry Finn by Mark Twain. I just loved the incredible voice of Huck and the whole romance of the epic raft journey.

How did you start writing?

I always loved writing at school. My school did a mini newspaper that went in the local newspaper. It was called *The Willowbank Warbler* and I did some sports reports. My first taste of success was getting picked for the last fifteen of a national writing competition.

What's your typical writing day?

I usually write twice a week for two to three hours each time.

What inspired you to write your book?

Jonny Jakes began life as a space pirate! I think the idea was simply to put two things together that I knew my sons would find interesting and see what happened.

What other jobs have you done?

Quite a few! Waiter, tree surgeon and care worker to name three. I am currently a teacher, but when I grow up I want to be an international film star.

What do you hope readers will think when they read your book?

I hope they laugh – a lot – but I also hope it will inspire the rebel in them and get them thinking about how to make a difference in their own world.

Is there anyone you would like to thank?

Penny West, my editor. This would not have happened without her.

EXCLUSIVE INTERVIEW

NAME:
Alan Brown

PROFESSION:
Illustrator

BIO:
Alan Brown's love of comic art, cartoons and drawing has driven him to follow his dreams of becoming an artist.

His career as a freelance artist and designer has allowed him to work on a wide range of projects, from magazine illustration and game design to children's books. He's had the good fortune to work on comics such as *Ben 10* and *Bravest Warriors*.

Alan lives in Newcastle with his wife, sons and dog.

Who's your favourite character to draw?

Without a doubt, Mr Jones.

Who's your favourite character overall?

Jonny – nothing stops him from getting to the truth.

Would you have joined Jonny's resistance group or would you not have been able to resist the sweets…?

I'm not a great fan of sweets, so I could have resisted. If they were alien pork pies, that would be a different story.

Do you think any of your teachers were secretly aliens?

Some of my teachers were almost certainly aliens, but others were so much worse than that.

What was your favourite book as a child?

My favourite books were *The Twits* by Roald Dahl, and a huge book on English folklore and myths my parents had. That's still my favourite book – it's really interesting to see where our traditions and beliefs come from.

How did you start illustrating?

I first got into illustration through doing storyboards for an ad agency. After many years working in graphic design, I've finally come back to my love of drawing. I've enjoyed working on a great many jobs over the past few years, but the highlights are definitely drawing the *Ben 10 Omniverse* comics and, of course, working on *Jonny Jakes*.

Do you sketch by hand or digitally?

It all depends on deadlines. If it's a tight timescale, I work completely digital. But if I have the time, I prefer to draw traditionally then work up the sketch digitally to create the final piece.

If you weren't an illustrator, what would you be and why?

Other than working as an illustrator, I've been a graphic designer and tattoo artist. But as a child I always wanted to be one of the guys who works in the lab for James Bond, making rocket pens and invisible shoes.

What's your typical working day?

I usually get up at 4.30 a.m., grab a coffee and start work. At 6.30 a.m. I walk the dog and make breakfast, then generally go back to work at 9 a.m. and work through until about 6 or 7 p.m. Long days but I get paid to draw aliens … can't complain!

JONNY JAKES

Investigates

THE OLD SCHOOL
GHOUL

It's been over a hundred years since head teacher Victory Piggot terrified his last pupil – but now he's back.

Sort of.

It's up to Jonny to get him to leave, before he unleashes unspeakable horrors on the school (including extra PE lessons).

HYPERSPACE HIGH

THE SCHOOL THAT'S OUT OF THIS WORLD

When John Riley catches the wrong bus, he ends up on Hyperspace High – an amazing school on a spaceship!

Light years from home, John makes friends with aliens, struggles through Galactic Geography lessons, and eats gross Martian food in the canteen.

But John needs to get up to speed fast, or he'll be booted back to Earth. Will an asteroid storm on a school trip give him a chance to prove that you don't have to be top of the class to be a hero?

READ THEM ALL!

ROBOT RACES

READY... STEADY... RACE!

Jimmy Roberts loves watching the Robot
Races, where drivers and their super-smart
talking robots compete. When a new race for
kids is announced, Jimmy is desperate to join.
There's only one hitch – he'll never be able
to afford a robot.

But then Jimmy's grandpa reveals he's turned
his battered old taxicab into a real-life robot!

Will Jimmy and his robot Cabbie ever be able
to keep up with the competition?

OUT NOW!

For more exciting books from brilliant
authors, follow the fox!
www.curious-fox.com